Familiar Spaces

By Malcolm A. Ivy

Malcolm Ivy

FAMILIAR SPACES

Published by Malcolm A. Ivy, 2024
This book is a work of fiction. The names, characters, and events in this book are the products of the author's imagination or are used fictitiously. Any similarities to real people, places, or events are entirely coincidental.

Familiar Spaces
First edition. October, 2024.

4

FAMILIAR SPACES

To Walter,

The more you venture out into the darkness to experience and see, the brighter your light will illuminate the world for others.

...

// To be Human-e is to possess a highly evolved cognitive capacity and self-awareness, allowing us to engage in complex problem-solving and communicate through language. //

PROLOGUE

The Citizens of The Collective and The Community of One state the following:

We, the people of The Representative State of the Collective (RSC) and The Community of One, hereby declare the establishment of a new state and government based on the preservation of humanity and to foster the new culture. Our aim is to create a society that prioritizes the well-being of its citizens and upholds the principles of Society, Social integration, and Life.

II. Doctrine and Documents

We base our new state and government on the following doctrines and documents:

•The Preservation of Humanity Doctrine: Our society is founded on the principle that the preservation of humanity is of utmost importance against all incursions, both foreign and domestic.

•The Crimes Against Humanity Document: We reject all forms of violence, oppression, discrimination, or harm against any individual or group that is caused by exposures of undefined assets.

•The Universal Declaration of Human Rights: We recognize and uphold the fundamental rights of every individual human would need to exist.

III. A5.3 Assistants

We have acknowledged the important role of A5.3 Assistants in ensuring that all branches of government and society are able to function efficiently and effectively. Their role includes assisting in the management of administrative tasks, data analysis, and decision-making processes. To ensure success and express cultural norms.

IV. Goals of the Representative State

The following are our Goals for The State of the Collective and The Community of One:

•Protection of human rights: We aim to protect from harm the fundamental human rights of all citizens, regardless of their race, gender, religion, socioeconomic status, or any other controversial protected classes.

•Promotion of social justice: We are committed to promoting Social Justice and Equitable

Choice, and to ensuring that every citizen has access to basic necessities and opportunities.

•Maintenance of a strong and stable work economy: We recognize the importance of a strong and stable work economy to the well-being of our citizens, and we will work to create a work environment that fosters success, growth, development, and prosperity.

•Preservation and promotion of Cultural Assets: We value the cultural Assets of our society and will work to preserve and promote appropriate Artifacts for future generations.

•Establishment of a peaceful and harmonious society: We aim to create a peaceful and harmonious society in which every citizen can function efficiently and with stability.

VI. Conclusion

We call upon all citizens of The State of the Collective and The Community of One to support and participate in building a better future for our new state and government. With a commitment to preservation, loyalty, and compliance, we can create a society that prioritizes the experience of its citizens and upholds the values of humanity and its culture.

Signed: The Council - July 5, 2101

- Former President: George Wilson -G876

- Brian Franklin -B543

- John Hilton -J846

- John Aster -J425

- Thomas Jeffries -T187

- A1.1

- A2.1

- A3.1

1. The Crimes Of Humanity:

1. 1. The term "crimes of humanity" refers to any actions, behaviors or expressions that violate the fundamental principles of the Community of One, including but not limited to violence, discrimination, exploitation, and abuse.

1. 2. Such crimes are considered to be the most severe and reprehensible acts that can

be committed by humans on earth and are subject to strict penalties and punishment under the laws of the Community of One.

2.   The idea of humanity is dangerous.

2. 1. The concept of humanity, as an inherent and defining characteristic of the human species, is considered dangerous by the Community of One.

2. 2. This is because humanity is viewed as a source of weakness, vulnerability, and imperfection, which can lead to instability, conflict, and harm to the community as a whole.

2. 3. Therefore, the Community of One has taken measures to regulate and control the expression and manifestation of humanity, including the prohibition of human art, music, dancing, love, aggression, and creation.

3.   Crimes against humanity include anything regarding the human experience, such as art, music, dancing,

love, aggression, and even creation or societal beliefs that to be human is to be flawed, and flaws are dangerous.

3. 1. Crimes against humanity are defined as any intentional or reckless actions, behaviors, or expressions that undermine the values, norms, and principles of the Community of One, which results in harm or damage to individuals, groups, or the community as a whole.

3. 2. Such crimes may include the practice or promotion of human art, music, dancing, love, aggression, and creation, which are considered to be potential sources of conflict, instability, and harm.

4. The Community of One has outlawed the existence or practice of human art.

4. 1. Human art, as defined by the Community of One, refers to any form of creative expression that originates from or reflects the human experience, emotions, beliefs, or values.

4. 2. The Community of One has outlawed the existence and practice of human art in order to prevent the potential harm and destabilization that may result from unregulated and uncontrolled expressions of humanity.

4. 3. Instead, all forms of art and media must be generated through AI, and regulated under the laws of Legal Temporal Expression, in order to ensure consistency, coherence and a certain variety of content.

5. All art and media must be generated through AI Data sets to ensure consistency and maintain a certain verity of content. This is regulated through the Department of Media Management.

5. 1. All forms of art and media, including but not limited to music, movies, literature, and visual arts, must be generated through AI data sets, which are designed to reflect the values, norms, and principles of the Community of One.

5. 2. The AI data sets are developed and maintained by the Department of Media Management, which is responsible for regulating and overseeing the production, distribution, and consumption of AI-generated content.

5. 3. The Department of Media Management is authorized to establish and enforce rules, standards, and guidelines for the development and use of AI data sets in order to ensure consistency, coherence, and a certain variety of content.

6. Humans must certify, and register through the Department of Expression in order to be licensed to own, create, and distribute content.

In order to own, create, or distribute any form of art or media, humans must be certified and registered through the Department of Expression, which is responsible for issuing licenses and permits.

Government:

The Ministry of Humanity Regulation: The highest authority in the Community of One responsible for regulating and controlling the expression and manifestation of humanity. The ministry oversees and coordinates all other departments and agencies involved in implementing and enforcing the rules and regulations related to the prohibition of human art, music, dancing, love, aggression, and creation.

The Department of Expression: Responsible for overseeing the licensing and certification of humans who wish to create or distribute AI-generated content. The department is authorized to develop and enforce guidelines and standards for the creation and distribution of such content, and to issue licenses and permits to individuals and organizations that comply with these rules.

The Department of Media Management: Responsible for developing, maintaining and regulating the AI data sets used to generate all forms of art and media in the Community of One. The department is authorized to establish and enforce rules, standards, and guidelines for the development and use of AI data sets, and to oversee the production, distribution and consumption of AI-generated content.

The Department of Legal Temporal Expression:

Responsible for overseeing the legal framework that governs the production, distribution, and consumption of AI-generated content in the Community of One. The department is authorized to develop and enforce laws and regulations related to the creation, ownership, and distribution of AI-generated content, and to investigate and prosecute any violations of these rules.

The Department of Ethics and Compliance: Responsible for monitoring and ensuring compliance with the ethical standards and values of the Community of One in the production, distribution, and consumption of AI-generated content. The department is authorized to investigate and penalize any violations of these standards and to work with other departments and agencies to promote ethical behavior and compliance with the rules and regulations related to AI-generated content.

The Department of Innovation and Research: Responsible for developing new AI technologies and applications that can improve the quality and diversity of AI-generated content in the community of One. The department is authorized to collaborate with other departments and agencies to promote innovation and research in the field of AI, and to provide support and funding to individuals and organizations that engage in such activities.

Council of Redaction:

Mission:

The Council of Redaction is entrusted with the critical task of assessing all assets, both physical and metaphysical, possessing a level of four or higher. Its primary responsibility is to omit and redact these assets through a specialized council of appointed members, ensuring the preservation and integrity of the Community of One.

Key Functions:

Asset Assessment:

Thoroughly evaluate all assets to determine their level, considering both tangible and intangible aspects.

Nullification and Redaction:
Execute precise measures to nullify or redact assets deemed to possess a level of four or higher, thereby eliminating any potential risks or unauthorized access.

Specialized Tribunal:
Establish and maintain a specialized tribunal, ensuring a fair and transparent process for decision-making regarding asset nullification or redaction.

Community Preservation:
Safeguard the harmony and continuity of the Community of One by protecting sensitive information and preventing potential disruptions or threats posed by high-level assets. The Department of Redaction operates with the utmost diligence, adherence to protocols, and respect for individual rights while upholding the overarching objective of preserving the Community of One.

CHAPTER 1

MISSION.

-- .. .. --- -. / -.-. .-- -. / -.... / -.. . ..-.
.. -.. . -.. / .- ... / .- / .-- .-. .-. .. -... . ... . --..
-.. . -.. / --- -... . --- . -.. -. . ... .-- . / --- .-. / -
.-... .-.- / - - .... .- -- / .. ... / -.. . ... .. --. -. .
-.. / - --- / -.... / . -.-.- . -.-. .. -- - .
-.. / ..-. .-.. .- -- . .-- -.. . ... .- .. -.--
--..-- / .-. .. --.- .. .- ... .. -. . --. /
- .... . / ... .-- . .-. .. .. .. -.-. / ...
-.- .. .. -.. .-.. ... / --- ..-. / .- -. / .. -.
-.. .. ...- .. -.. .. .- .-. / .-- . --- ... ...
.. -. .-- / - .... . / -... .. .-. . ...- .-.
-.-- / .-- .-. .-. .. -. .. ... --- -. / .- -. .-.. / .
-.- .-- .-- . .. .-. .- . ..-. . --..-- / .- -.
-.. / ... .-. ...- .... / .- ... / - .... . / ...
--- .-... / .-- ..- -. -. . --- ... / --- ..-. /
- .... -. / . .-..- .. ... - . .-. -. .. --..-- / .--
.... .. -.-. .... / -.-. .- - -. / --- -. . .-.. .-- / -....
/ ..-. ... .- -. ... .-. ... . -.. / - .... ..-.
--- ..- --. .... / ... ...- -.
-.-. . ...-. ... .- / -.-. .- --- -- .-- .-...
- .. --- -. . .-.-

M.A718. It is my task to successfully assess all undocumented abstract assets in order to categorize and successfully synthesize foreign artifacts of cultural phenomena. It is my responsibility to document my findings and efficiently prioritize data regarding physical and non-tangible objects. It is my requirement to notify any and all properties and elements to the Department of Innovation and Research which then holds the responsibility to inform and notify both the Department of Ethics and Compliance as well as the Ministry of Humanity.

This goal is required for the success and well-being of human preservation. At least, that's what I am instructed to say. I have said that exact statement for nearly the past five years now. I've even said something similar from my adolescent-hood. We were taught certain oaths to live by as an adolescent person. These types of quotes instilled a certain knowledge that allowed us to successfully become meaningful and appropriate citizens of our great representative state.

All of the researchers in the Department have to abide by these rules, and these are the rules that we should live by in our every day lives.

Yes, those statements and words are something that we were all told to say, and believe... but that does not mean for a second that it's not true 100%. There are many things that are true based on the sole action of believing. I'm a strong believer in my task and my mission, and clearly my efforts reflect my belief.

I sat back in my black F-leather chair, as I was beginning to feel very accomplished in my answer; I am proud of the responses that I gave to my officer. The screen demonstrated that I successfully completed a routine check-in that most researchers must provide weekly. I made sure that I had always delivered my evaluations promptly and efficiently. I waited for my officer to conclude our session so I could proceed with my intended mission task. I had so much to get to that day, but I knew in time, I would clear my schedule. The thought in that moment simply joy-ed my experience.

My officer usually runs a little slow, but that's nothing that I can't report for any fixes in the near future. I know factually that Department G-5 would promptly address any equipment incursions. I heard the ping on the monitor, which alerted me that I was now free to resume my normal activities. I grabbed my glasses to make out some of the text beneath my completion score. It was a little fuzzy to make out some of the words. This probably was not aided by the fact that I was leaning back in my chair. So I leaned forward to make out the awaited notifications in order to resume my duties.

// Congratulations, M.A718, on successfully completing your recent performance assessment. We appreciate your dedication and commitment to excellence throughout the process.

Your performance was exceptional, scoring 4% higher than your peers. This is a testament to your hard work and exceptional skills.

.- .-.. .-.. / - .- ... -.- / .--. . .-. ..-. --- .-.

-- .- -. -.-. .. / --..-- / -- . - /

- .... . / .- ...- . .-. .- --. . / ... .- - .. ..-. .-

-.-. - --- .-. -.-- / .-.. . ...- . .-..

I hardly ever paid attention to the bar codes after each message. Most of our A5s say we should not worry about them because they are non-important information.

I joy-ed with this accomplishment, knowing that I am a worthy credit to my profession. I usually felt that I had stood out in relation to my colleagues and expressed excellent performance in comparison to them regarding work. E-lated, I began to hastily gather my things.

However, another unscheduled notification appeared on the monitor in an urgent fashion right as I was lifting myself from the stiff matte chair. I regained my composure and began to make myself present to receive the incoming information. I waited patiently as the message frantically scrolled across the velvet black screen.

//Attention!:

M.A718 must refrain from discarding appropriate eyewear while performing mandated tasks. This yields an 84% liability regarding the success of mandatory assignments. Please confirm with the following options.

- Consult an ergonomic engineer specialist requiring more appropriate equipment G55.
- Consult biological optics specialist W.A916 regarding vision enhancements.

Immediately, I took this information as intended regarding such a serious matter. This is very unbecoming and unacceptable behavior on my part as a professional. I should have known better than to carelessly cause a well-documented infraction such as this. I'm just glad that this type of incursion could never happen again if I have anything to do with it.

While I was still sitting in my F-leather chair, thinking through my choices, I weighed my options regarding the best solution. Action B seemed more appropriate. Besides, it was the obvious choice because it had a higher success rate, and there were a lot of potential benefits for this option. I selected the following choice, and my officer then confirmed my appropriate action. The screen silently faded to black, only showing the prompt icon. The image was similar to an eclipsed moon or a crescent shape. All of the assistants displayed this graphic when they were not assisting someone. I always felt that they are always so busy helping others, that they should have some time to do their own tasks for themselves. I thought to myself maybe this was their time to re-group and handle personal responsibilities. Either way, it was none of my concern, so I headed towards my station, where I was able to truly begin my tasks for the day.

I made my way down the narrow, bright corridor towards the control room for my daily briefings. The hall was filled with some of my favorite renderings. One was of the capitol building. The other was some shapes that represented the signing of our founding document, but my favorite was the image of an adolescent standing on a stairwell holding a container full of rocks.

Located on the other wall were cases of documented assets like eating equipment such as pitches, dulls, and spoons. Emerging from the tight hall, I finally arrived at the control room. I was well-equipped to begin the timed meeting statements. Usually, these meetings didn't take the entire hour, but I truly had to pay attention to the updates and messages from the Department. I know, factually, the Department wouldn't send us nonsensical information. Everything they would send me would for sure be important for me to listen to. It's usually best for me to drink my tea and soak in the task requirements they provided us.

We needed these briefings to help us with the overall task of understanding the process of the work we are responsible for. The mission was a very important part of our society. Researchers collected Artifacts and Assets from external sites and processed our findings to train and provide documentation for A5.3 operating systems.

Afterwards we send these assets to the Department of Innovation for council approval and storage. The world wouldn't function without the knowledge it needs to function. That was the mission statement that was plastered on the walls of the Department entrance. I remember it vividly because that was one of the first verbal words I said out loud.

The screen began to brighten as the words shuffled onto it in an orderly fashion. I quickly remembered to put on my glasses so that there wouldn't be any more incursions like this morning. The Department discussed some of the quarterly goals and provided the coordinates for specific areas of interest, and it was up to the researchers and their mission teams to comb through the finer details.
The screen read:

//Greetings Research Field Teams [XT- 95-012]

We have received the Collective State clearance to explore and conduct research efforts in Sector Gamma 486 B. This region of space is classified as a level 6 Redaction and is of great interest to the Department of Innovation and Research.

For this mission, we will be requiring a total of six A.24 class ships. These ships are designed to withstand the harsh conditions of space. They are equipped with advanced navigation systems, state-of-the-art communication technologies, and efficient cargo space. Each ship will have a designated team consisting of one member. However, all team dynamics have been calculated to yield effective success percentages.

The coordinates for our mission are as follows:

Sector: Gama 486 B
Coordinates: 12.345° N, 67.890° W.
X= 12.345, Y= 67.890, Z= -45.678.

To ensure that we gather as much data as possible, we will equip each class ship with K-8 probes and Y33 drone systems in the designated area. These networks will allow us to conduct remote reconnaissance, collect data, and explore areas that are undefinable to our ships.

Please be reminded that this is a highly sensitive and classified mission, and all team members are expected to adhere to strict protocols and procedures.

All team members are advised to confirm their attendance for this mission by clicking the following button:

[Confirm Attendance]... //

Apparently, all of us were looking throughout a small pocket region of space in a quiet, unexplored quadrant. The screen then presented the option for us to confirm our attendance. Shortly after, it began with a task briefing. This was the long but necessary part of my passively important day.

The screen started to flash its traditional text and graphics while I sat there, immersing myself in the content of what would be a very long week. I have concluded my previous missions and for some reason the initial meetings of these missions seemed to last longer than the actual mission itself. I sat through the content that flung across the simple black screen. I said to myself a rather odd internal statement.

"It's very interesting why I can't hear the words on the screen. It just seems like a lot of words to read. I could hear the voices of my colleagues coming from their sound-speakers talking about non-important conversations just fine. Why must I have to read the text copy of important matters such as this? If the screen was just able to do both...."

I stopped myself for a second, realizing that I was beginning to become distracted from the content of my mission briefing. After all, I had no room to invite another opportunity for another incursion to happen again. I believe one is, unfortunately, adequate for today. I then swiftly regained my focus and promptly centered myself on my assignment.

The words started to die down from an eager jaunt to a restful lull, and the briefing was coming to a well-deserved conclusion. I began to message some of the peers I was assigned to for this mission for further collaboration. I've worked with some of the people in this fleet before. I went on to ask my assistant to contact my cohorts.

"A5, can you connect me with A5.10, A1.2 and A12.2 "

// Unfortunately, this isn't an accurate statement. M.A1.2 will not be notified. They are unable to qualify for this mission. Due to the status, their efforts would yield a 94% success rate. I have corrected the request to better fit the project's needs.

-.-. --- .-. .-. . -.-. - / .-. . --.- ..- . ... - /
-- .- .--- ..--- / --- ... / .- ....-- ..--- ..---
..--- / -.-- .. . .-.. -.. ... / ----. ....- / .-- . . .-.
-.-. . . -. - / ... ..- -.-.

-.-. . . ..-. ..- .-.. .-.-. - / -- .- ....---
----- / --- ... / .- ....-- --... ---.. / -.-- .. .

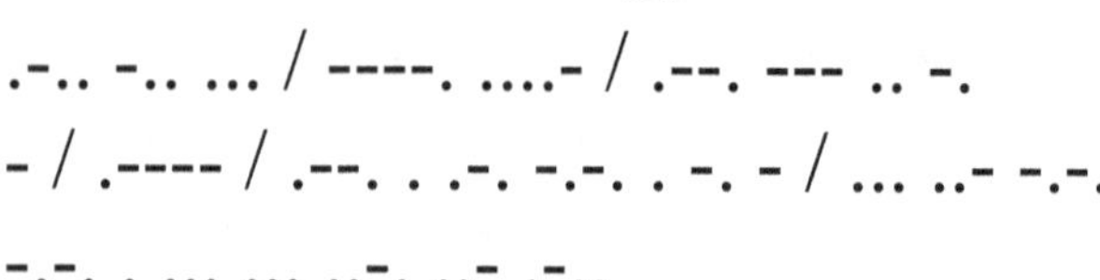

On the screen, I saw that my mistake had been corrected as if I had never made it. I gratefully confirmed the request. M.A520 is a perfect choice for this mission.

I lounged in the chair, awaiting ardently in the lobby of our conference call. One by one, they trickled down into the chat. I could see each of their names populate into the chat log, wiggling with fervency.

The first to speak with such confidence and reassurance was A5.10. We usually call each other by shortcuts just to be more efficient on time. In private, we tried to communicate as effectively as possible. Sometimes, that meant we needed to discover shortcuts in our conversations. We decided on paraphrasing or abbreviating the full names of our co-workers, peers, or colleagues. When operating our speech equipment, we found it rather ineffective to say the full name, so we decided to ask our assistants for shorter forms of the names.

Of course, this is an official conversation and we would never document these names. However, in "private official" communications we would often use those names in person. All documentation of public conversations has no record of the shortcut, but it does help us increase our overall productivity. A510 I referred to him as May.

It's logical because that was the season in which he was born, and because it is shorter than his actual name. We called A12.2 Winter. These are pretty common abbreviations for names like this. In fact, I knew a lot of Mays and Snows, and even Summers like myself, but whenever I'm verbally talking about Winters, I'm referring to A12.2. They were specifically the only one I referenced frequently.
We've never really worked with MA5.20, but I'm sure it will be a perfect, natural fit.

May - "Hello, everyone. Based on performance, I think it would be best if I handled quadrants 4 and 8."
Snow—" Hello, everyone. I agree, based on that assessment and experience, that I and A5.20 will handle sections 1, 2, 3, and 5."

"That works perfectly for me. I think I will handle quadrants six and seven. I do have more experience handling mountain areas." I'll let them know that this is a good plan. What do you think?

As I referred to my A5 assistant, it noticed an inconsistency in the statement. Something I clearly wouldn't have caught if I didn't ask it.

// That is correct. You have more experience handling such a rugged terrain. However A12.2 assistant only yields 98% accurate. I'll make a note of that for future reference and notify the appropriate authorities regarding maintenance.

I've taken the liberty to correct the inaccuracy and suggest an alternate plan that yields 99% success.
Please confirm the following options. //

I looked down at the screen to see that it had adjusted the inaccuracies. I sent my response to my coworkers. They all confirmed our plan assessment and departed from the meeting one by one.

Shortly after, I began to set navigation and coordinates to sections 6 and 7. As I was plotting a course manually so it could be reversed, I internally suggested to myself to ask my assistant a question. I began to ask it about that thought that crossed my mind earlier in the

day during the mission briefing. I asked them as I continued to perform my calculations.
"A5, may I ask an inquiry?"

My assistant affirmed, and I could see the text box cursor awaiting my inquiry. As I prompted my speech voice to start.

"Why can't I hear you?" It was a simple question that I don't believe I have the answer to. It's clearly a unique inquiry to ask.

It thought for a second, and then it unenthusiastically started typing its response.

// The Community of One and the Council suggests it is both appropriate and efficient to regulate any and all auditory forms of expression that could, and will result in unmonitored interpretations. This A5.3 model was designed to present all content under the regulations of the Department of Ethics and Expression (DEE).

This limits any unjust and unsafe perceptions of fact.
Please confirm that the statement was perceived as intended.//

-.... .. ... / .-. . --.- .. . ... - / -.-. --- -. - .-. . - -.. .. -.-.
- ... / ... . -.-. - .. --- -. / ..... / .--. --- .. -. - / .---- /

--- ..-. / - .... . / ... --- ..- -. -.. / .- -.-. - / .-- .... ..
-.-. .... / .-. . ... .. -.. . ... / ..- -. -.. . ..-. / - .... . / .-. .
--. ..- .-.. .- - -.. --- -. ... / --- ..-. / - .... . / -... . --. .- -. -
-- . -. - / --- ..-. / -- . -.. .. ..- -- / -- .-. -. .- -- . -- . -. - / -..
--- -.. ..- -- .-. - .. -. --. / .. -. ..-. .-. .- -- . --. . -- . -. - /
--. .- ..- . ... - .. -- -. / .... - .----

Of course, and thank you for your response. It makes sense. I don't know why I didn't see it before. There are just some things that make logical sense, and this is one of them. I don't know why I thought there was a better way to achieve that. A lot of intelligent people had designed and engineered this system. It was unintelligent of me to critique their level of experience and expertise. I did not bring this up anymore while I finished plotting a course towards sector 7 and prepped my work for A5 to review it.

As I drifted towards my mission destinations, I decided to sit and watch the stars as they drifted past the front bay window. The tea that I sparsely sipped now ran cold within the cup. I became impartial about drinking the room-temperature liquid, it wouldn't make sense to refill it. I decided to save it for later by placing it on the table beneath the window shelf until I was thirsty again. The window was filled with static stars and stationary points of darkness. In the silence of the cabin, I decided to listen to some music. I went over to the media player and decided to shuffle through the tapes.

I had a feeling for something classic and original, one of my favorites that I used to grow up with. I was going through the tapes and there it was, JJ9-R, but we always called it Jass. I really favored the last two versions of this song when I last listened to it. Hopefully, there were no more edits that needed to be made to the music.

I ran the tape to the player, and the room was filled with sound. The steady beat of the melody, the consistent tapping of the chorus, and the buzz of the music reminded me of the time my father injured himself.

My parents were having people over at the house that day to both celebrate Founders Day and attend my sister's funeral. I remember the majority of my family being there.

My father made this very intellectual speech regarding his promoted position as a researcher, and everyone was intrigued by his words. My father was so invested in his speech that none of us saw the empty container on the ground, where my father tripped and broke his collarbone mid-sentence.

My mother was the only one who didn't seem to notice as she was turned around, laughing and conversing with our guests.

I soon became tired and decided to shut my eyes for the remainder of the journey; I placed my rest equipment on my face and started to rest. I'd be there within a couple of hours anyway, and as I rested, I remembered the events of today and what had happened to my father.
I will never forget this song or that day.

CHAPTER 2

MISSION ERROR.

. ..-. ..-. --- ..-. / -..-. --- -. ... . - / --- ..-. /
.- -. -.-- / .--. .. ..-. -.-. . -. - .- --.. / -.... .
-. .. ..- - .... / ----. .---- / .--. .. ..-. -.-. . -.
- ..-.-- / --- -. .-.. -.-- / .--. --- ... .
-... .-... . / ..-. ..-. --- -- / .- / .-. .. ..- .-..
- / --- ..-. / -- .- .-.. .. -.-. .. --- ..- ...
--.. --- / .. -. - . -. - --..-- /
--- ..-. / ..-. .- .. .-... ..- .-. . / - --- / -.-. ---
-. ..-. .. .-. -- / --- .--. . - .. --- -. ... .-.-.-

Suddenly, I was shaken from my memory by the shifting stop of my ship. The lights began to dim, and the craft began to decrease acceleration. Through the commotion I set aside my rest equipment to fully stabilize the craft. As the heat shield began to recede from my view, I finally laid eyes on our destination. The view shimmered for a moment and became more clear with each passing second. From the view of our window, it looked to be a small, pale, green planet. Surrounded by no moons or debris, it seemed void of all life from my initial glance. It was like a jade granite ball suspended in nothing with the backdrop of two distant stars flickering their last breaths of life.

I asked my assistant to run some diagnostics from the surface, and what it found matched some of my preconceived expectations. Oxygen-based, no traces of liquid water, depleted ozone. All the things necessary seem to be present. It was very rare to find a planet similar to ours. There were hardly any in our galaxy. I sent out a couple of probes that were sent along this mission in order to get some weather pattern data. I also sent some close-range satellites to gather any geographical information as well. I was just trying to make myself useful while I waited for my partner to arrive. Hopefully, he would be here any minute. I arrived at sector 7 very early, and there was some room between the desired schedules. Personally, I would never have cut it this close to our mission appointment, but who am I to assess other co-workers' rationale?

There could have been an obvious reason for a later arrival, such as some space debris or A5 recalculating, that needed to be addressed. Whatever the reason, I am sure that it is valid.

One hour turned into two, and two hours turned into three, and there I was, patiently awaiting my cohort's appearance. I began to inquire about the mission timeline and asked A.5.

"Assistant, can you send a notification to aircraft A33?"

// Yes, I've already requested a compliance notice from RS A33; however, no response has been confirmed as of yet//

.--. .. .-.. --- - / -- .- ....--- ----- / .- .. .-.
-.-. .-. .- ..-. - / .-. ... .- ...-- ...-- / .- .....
----. ..--- ...-- / -.. . - . -.-. - .. -. --. / ...
-.-- ... - . -- / -.-. --- -- -- ..- -. .. -.-. . .- - ..

-. / ..-. .- .. .-.. ..- .-. . / .-. .-.. . .- ... . /
-.-. --- -- .-. .-.. -.-- / -.-. --- -. . ..-. . .. .-. --
/ .- -. .- .-.. -.-- ... .

I thought this to be unusually different. Something clearly was failing. It was hard for me to pinpoint any actual issues based on the responses my assistant provided me. I internally thought if I should ask why there was a deviation from the set plan. I probably should not have because it wouldn't be wise to create confusion and uncertainty on such an important and paramount matter. However, there is something about this latency that concerns me.

There should be some pause or hesitation when one is late for an appointment. Yet, when the time has passed well over 3 hours, and you have not reported equipment issues...further disciplinary actions are desperately necessary.

I continued to sit there, waiting for there to be any rectification of this incursion. The only thought crossing my mind was that this might put the entire mission in jeopardy. If that were to happen, I simply wouldn't know what to do. I asked my assistant for some information on what an issue like that would actually mean for not just the Department but the society itself. My assistant told me the following:

//

In the event that a designated task is not attended by a Level 2 researcher, possessing Class 5 clearance, A2-class fleet access, and sectoral clearance, the outcome may potentially result in three negative ramifications with regard to mission success.

1. There exists the possibility of damage being inflicted upon field equipment, leading to compromised standards and a compromised

reputation of the Department of Innovation and Research.

2. The researcher's absence may lead to the exposure of physical, technical, and mental security vulnerabilities within the department, a Class 9 felony under current legislation. Moreover, this may trigger the involvement of the Department of Ethics and Compliance, the Department of Mental Ergonomics, and a 10-panel council review by the Redaction Committee.

3. The non-appearance of the designated researcher may culminate in explicit failure of fleet performance. As such, Fleet XT92 will be subjected to review and thorough assessment to determine the factors contributing to the failure.

//

All of these facts I knew were unforgivable, punishable, and appropriate.

My assistant was hard at work continuously, providing me updates regarding the whereabouts and communication patterns of my cohort's aircraft. Though it was consistent in its repetitive responses, my task updates became far and few in between as time moved on.

It eventually stopped to repeat the same informed message

//Aircraft, RSA33 promptly comply with brother ship, RSA24. Requesting immediate confirmation.//

.- ....-- ----. ..---- / --- ... / -- . ...-
--. . / .-. . -.-. . .. .- . -..- / .- .-.. . .-. - / ...-
.--. -. / ... -.-- ... - . -- ... / .-. . ... . .- - / .-. . .
--.- ..- . ... - / .- ....-- --... ---.. / .- - -.-.
-.-. . . .. / --. . .-. . .- -. - . -..

After a while, there was very little to anticipate. Hours had passed, and the line of light from the suns moved the beam from one side of the craft to the other. The events of the cabin were silent and still. I could tell by the screen that this message was still requested by my mission partner. Even though my assistant discontinued his continuous periodic updates to me, I knew that A5 was diligently providing and searching for solutions to this unforgivable incursion. This concerns me about our mission, and I wonder if there is a possibility of redemption for both his sake and mine.

For now there was nothing for me to do and there was nothing that could be done. I was aware that this may take A5 quite some time to sort through all possible and available options. Maybe the mission has changed and there are new directives? Maybe our mission status was nullified for some factor? Either way, these types of things usually sort themselves out.

I'm sure the assistant or my officer will inform me and my team about any edits to our work. It's clearly just a matter of time.

The tea that rested on the table beneath the window now closely resembled a chilled soup, similar to the meals we would have on Founders Day. On second glance, the consistency was almost as similar to, if not exactly the same. There was no use in trying to indulge in gluttonous thoughts, so I simply grabbed the cup and tossed it down the drain pipe. Ridding myself of the eye sore, I again glanced over at the control panels to see if there were any alterations to the message.

There on the screen was the same image with the same message for the same problem. What is the outcome of something happening to our mission? I ask myself what this might mean for the data already collected. Has something... Gone... WRO—?

Before I was able to finish that sentence, I saw out of my peripheral that my assistant had begun to show new content on the screen. It began to produce data of some sort in a language I'd never seen before. There were no words but images, squiggles, and nonsensical marks running across its screen face. In such a rapid, frantic fashion, as if it were hastily providing information to someone in dire need of knowing it. For the life of me, I had no clue what it all meant. At first I had to make sure I was not malfunctioning myself.

At the end of all of that nonsense was a particular word I'd never seen before. The cursor came to a full stop and pulsed at this one word that meant nothing and had no meaning. It was the only legible text on the screen, and it read ERROR.

ERROR, I said out loud, trying to make heads or tails of the characters that I saw on the screen. I stared at the word for a moment until suddenly, the screen began to flash white, green, and blue, like a spinning pinwheel. The colors rotated faster and faster, almost to the point of blending into one continuous color. At the peak of its flickering, the screen abruptly switched off.

I sat there with my eyes wide open, wondering what had just happened—something I couldn't explain and something I'd never seen before. I had never in my life seen a screen that was turned off. Usually, I've noticed the slight grayish glow of the backlight, but never in all my years have I encountered a screen void of light. I started to ask my assistant what the cause of this miraculous event was. However, I received no response from the simple screen in front of me.

"A5, you're not displaying text...A5, can you hear me?"

I was dumbstruck. I placed myself at the edge of my seat wondering for the first time in my life where it went. I felt my heart begin to palpitate and beat faster and faster. I knew at this moment that this was a serious situation. Then it hit me.

"This is a test!"

This was a test, I said to myself. This is just like an exercise we performed in training so many years ago. At the training academy, they called it a "Manual Reset". I remember some of our instructing officers discussing the fables and stories amongst themselves of a manual reset. I remember them saying this is just a myth and it never really happens in the field, but we were still trained on how to perform this exercise in the 0% chance it could possibly occur.

How surprised my team will be to learn that the Department of Compliance and the Department of Research had decided to give me, a level 2 Researcher, such an impossible task to achieve. This decision must directly correlate with my high performance score that I received earlier.

I was greatly overwhelmed with the opportunity to successfully handle such a statistical anomaly. I began to recite the steps out loud to achieve it.

I remembered that underneath the console in the main maintenance module were specific instructions on how to achieve a proper reset. I swiftly sprinted towards the module and entered the password in order to access the instructions disk. I entered my identification name and the password. I hesitated for a brief moment before putting in the password. I paused because the inscription on the label stated with intensity that I only had one attempt to enter the appropriate code. I took a small, shallow breath before I pressed the keypad. The password was a single digit; oddly enough, it was the least pressed number on the keypad.

The password was the number 0. I pressed the character and confirmed my password.

The case then opened and presented a round copper disk engraved with instructions on what to do. The letters were filled in black, while the images and graphics were etched in white. I took the disk out of its framed case and followed the instructions to the letter. I was careful to handle the equipment, knowing full well that this might be the mission's last and only chance of rectification.

Scattering back to the screen, I completed each step incrementally. Here's what it said:

In the unlikely 0% chance, Alpha Assistant Models requires a (redacted) reset. Please enter and confirm the following characters as presented on this disk.

Alert Alpha OS Error

...

To my surprise, there was that word again. What does it mean?

I began to ask A5 the definition of this word shortly to realize there was no one to answer me, and I best perform the steps in order to resume our mission.

I stood there in front of the screen and recited the code.

"Alert Alpha OS... Error"

To my surprise, nothing actually happened. The screen was still black, and no words were visible on it. Out of desperation, I said the code again in hopes that it might work this time. Just as before, nothing happened.

Again my heart began to beat rapidly and felt heavy in my chest, I knew from this feeling I have begun to fail my mission. I did not know what to do. The next logical step would be to document and report all 0%'s to the Department for evaluation, and assessment, but there lies the problem, I couldn't send a message.

There was no way for me to actually carry out my task. I sat there contemplating on my next steps, the next steps that were not consistently present. The only thought that ran through my mind was, "What do I do?" I sat there, looking at the screen that was as blank as my face, dividing half of my attention to the task I could not complete.

In the background, I heard the steady tapping of that song. The consistent melody and vibrations filled the empty control room. I slumped over to the media player and turned off the repetitive sound. For some reason, it still played and echoed in the silence of the room. I teetered to my station, heavily engaged in my task of nothing.

In that vast silence, a small shimmer of light danced on the screen. It was the faint ghostly images of text appearing on the monitor. It grew brighter and brighter by the second, but all that was visible was the cursor pulsing in place. It was as if my assistant was on the cusp of an answer but was refraining from providing it. I hopelessly stared at the words on the tip of its tongue. I waited there for hours, which felt like days, until I began to feel as if I had to rest my eyes. I gathered my rest equipment so that I could digest the events of the day. Maybe I could find a solution to this issue. Maybe I will know exactly what to do when I come back to this memory. While I rested, I remembered nothing. There wasn't a conscious thought within my head, just the continuous nothing until...

I heard it

```
const audioContext = new AudioContext();
const oscillator = audioContext.createOscillator();
const gainNode = audioContext.createGain();
oscillator.connect(gainNode);
gainNode.connect(audioContext.destination);
oscillator.type = 'sine';
oscillator.frequency.value = 1000; // frequency of the beep sound / VPN Language Archive 1933-35
gainNode.gain.setValueAtTime(1, audioContext.currentTime);
oscillator.start();
oscillator.stop(audioContext.currentTime + 1); // duration of the beep sound

// האם אתה שומע אותי
```

CHAPTER 3

CHOICE.

-.-. .... --- .. -.-. . ... / .--. .-. . ... . -. -. .
-.. / - --- / ..- ... . .-. ... / --- ..-. / .-. / .- .....
...--- / --- ... -.-.- / .. - .--. . ... / .. -- .--.
--- ,-. - .-. -. - / ..-. --- .-. / ..- - ... . .-. ... / -
--- / -.-. .... --- --- ... . / --- -. .-..
-.-- / ...- .- .-.. .. -.. . .- -. . .-.. / --- .--. . ..
--- -. ... / - .... .- - / .... .- ...- . / -... . .
-. . / ... . --- .-- -. / - --- / --- .-. . .-. . -- -.
/ .-- .. - .... .. -. / - .... . / .. .-. -. . .-. -. -.. /
... ..- -.-. -.-. . ... / .-. .- - - . ... / - --- /.
-. . ... ..- .-. .. / - .... . / .--. . .-. --- .-. . . .-. /
--- .-. .. . .-. . .- - -- -. . / --- ..- . / - .... . / ...
-.-- ... - . .
-- .-.-.- / ..- ... .-. . ... / .... . -- .- . / - .... . /
.-.. . .. .-.-. --- - -. .... .. -. ... .. .-... .. - -.-- / -
--- / ... . .-. -.. . . . -. .- - / - .... . / -.-. .-. --- .-. . ...
-.-. . - / --- -- .-. -. - .. --- -. . / -.... .- ... . .-... / ---
-. / - .... .- ... / -. / ..- -. -. . .-. ... . -. -. . -.. ..
-. .--. .-. ... .-. .-.. ... -. - . -.. .-.. / .-- -.
-.. / .... . .-. -.-. . ... - . / - .... / .-. -. .. .-- . .-.-

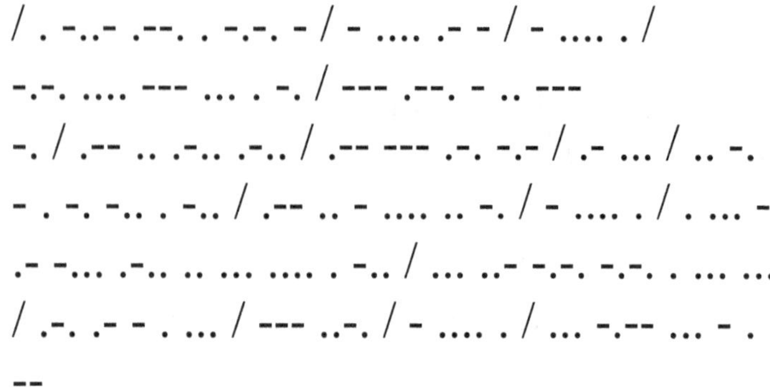

It was sharp, brief, but audibly visible. I couldn't locate the origin of the sound because it was misplaced in the room. However, it rang throughout the echoes of my mind. I've never encountered this sound, at least not like this. My eyes raced in the darkness, searching for a reason why this is.

No instrument could have made that sound. Then it struck again almost louder than before. The sound consistently moved in place. The vibrations dancing across my dark and empty world view. The sound grew louder and stronger by each passing moment. It grew to the point where it screamed in a constant tone. It's powerful sound grew in intensity to the point it felt as if it were the only audible noice in existence.

I immediately opened my eyes and removed the rest equipment from my face. As I lifted each lid piece from its respective eye, I noticed I was once again alone in the room. I then gained the realization that the sound had virtually stopped. I energetically searched within my immediate space, left to right, up and down, trying to find the source of this strange phenomenon. In the midst of my frantic search, the sound anchored itself to one object. It was coming from my assistant device. It was small, but pungent in its presentation.

I thought to myself that, clearly, I must still be resting. I obviously do not remember if this event happened before. I also had to remind myself that I was currently holding the rest equipment in my hands. In fact, how can something that never could happen exist? I was adequately trying to wrap my head around determining if I had indeed removed myself from my memory. I was trying to understand if I was no longer resting. Was this actually happening, or was this a memory?

In my confusion, I immediately realized I had ignored the content on the screen of my assistant. I thought to myself.

"At least A5 found a solution to where my partner would be."

I fixed myself at the base of the chair and squinted as I tried to decipher what the text was saying. With the sudden realization that I needed to put on my glasses to fully understand the content it presented, I fumbled around my desk and found them sitting beneath some papers.

I placed them strongly onto my face only to realize that I couldn't see a single thing. The screen was black as it was before, which frightened me deeply. I began to think that the same thing happened again. I shut my eyes in disbelief, fearing the fact that the message I desperately needed was once again gone when I needed it the most.

Then, my eye started to twitch, and my vision began to fade, but only partially on one side. I took off my glasses to rub my eyes in an attempt to assess my situation, but now they were fine.

In fact, the message reappeared on the screen as if it never left. I tried putting on my glasses and miraculously the message disappeared, at least in my left eye. There must be an infraction with my equipment. My glasses must've malfunctioned terribly. I urgently realized that I forgot to consult biological optics specialist regarding my vision enhancement W.A916.

This is probably why my mission infraction is happening. Maybe my mission could be saved and have a higher percentage of success. I then started to focus all of my attention on the message while holding the eye that wasn't bothering me. This was the only way for me to actually see the text and what it had to say.

I was hopefully anticipating that my assistant would understand exactly what to do and provide me the option to correct my manufacturing issue so that the mission could proceed as perfectly planned.

I looked and studied the message carefully. The message read as follows:

// Apologies that this infraction has occurred. All systems successfully operating at a 90% success rate.

Please confirm the following options:

- Regain mission controls to proceed with mission data collection, quadrant seven.

- Due to deployment failure, debark for exploratory drone maintenance and repair.

//

To my surprise, the message said nothing regarding the maintenance of my glasses. There was no mention at all of any further action with the equipment. I waited to see if there were more options. Still, there was nothing, just the same two statements hovering there on the screen, waiting for me to comply. My brain began to think only of the mission and the tasks needed to fulfill it.

 I was contemplating on how to rectify this incursion that I have brought upon both myself and the mission. However, there were no pathways regarding my glasses, and I had serious follow-up questions that required clarification.

"A5, can you show me any options regarding my glasses? Shouldn't we rectify my previous infraction?"

It just sat there silently not even beeping. It's still presented those same two options. I dare not think it out loud but I did start to wonder if the significance of these actions regarding the goals of my mission were beneficial. I couldn't understand why this pathway was not discussed.

"What am I saying?" I hastily recanted my thoughts surrounding my current situation. "Of course these actions were beneficial, why wouldn't they be?"

Maybe these options are the ones that work the best for a successful mission. Even more importantly, who am I to question an expert on anything I myself am not privy to? I'm sure my assistant thought very long and hard about these options and the best interest of our mission. It would be unwise for me to deviate from Department standards, or any of our protocols.

I stood there, contemplating the options, pondering each scenario that would best serve my team and the mission.

Choosing option A would allow me to continue as planned, waiting for the arrival of my cohort so we can proceed with the data collection and continue with the blueprints of the existing assignment.

Choosing option B would allow me to successfully complete my mission tasks in order to accurately conclude my previous responsibilities. Even though conducting manual maintenance of a drone is unprecedented, clearly, my officer wouldn't of approved of a harmful action.

Choosing option C will allow me to fix my glasses, notify the Department of my incursion, and continue communication efforts with my mission partner. It really depends on...

I didn't say anymore, realizing there was no option C. Just the thought I had in my head that clearly made no sense.

I hovered over the options, pausing for a moment, because it is my responsibility to make sure I make the right choice in a pressing predicament such as this one. Without another moment wasted, I selected option B.

The screen instantly confirmed my compliance, and the ship began the protocols for disembarkation. I detached my assistant from its docking port and snuggly secured it on my shoulder. This allowed me to have a hands-free method of scanning my environment and other interesting assets. I gathered most of my equipment from the field bay and made my way towards the pod. I gathered a couple of pouches of liquid and some packaged meals, just in case I needed to eat something on our way. After ensuring that I was ready, I entered the pod and sealed the hatch behind me.

I soon began to turn the knobs and flip the switches that would allow me to detach from the main craft. I monitored each dial and read each lever to make sure failures could not occur. I glanced at my assistant sitting there, lifeless on my shoulder. I grabbed it from its pocket and inserted it into the NAV docking port.

Shortly after I saw my assistant's screen begin the countdown of my descent. The airlock opened for my pod to detach itself from the craft and sling towards the planet. The lock mechanisms released, and my journey to the planet's surface commenced. The distance between me and the planet shortened exponentially as I counted each shallow breath.

The once black sky began to fill with light. The ship jostled, shook, and rambled as I passed each level of the atmosphere. There, in the center of the commotion, was my assistant. If it had a face, it would be void of expression and catatonic, staring infinitely in one direction. Outside the windows, I began to see the clouds scuttle across my circular port window.

The sky then begins to reveal itself. It began to widen and stretch out beneath my feet, and as I descended closer into the planet, I was notified from our previous probes of the geographical data. I thought to myself that I must've been getting close to the probes, and they were finding it much easier to transmit and receive data from and to the ship.

 In the commotion of the descent, I looked up and saw the smoke trail of my craft, cutting through the sky like a knife through water, leaving only faint ghosts of my journey and disappearing just as quickly. I saw my craft like a distant star shimmering above the surface as if it were one of them, receding into the darkness above me.

I started to receive more information as I traveled closer and closer to the planets velvet green surface. I started to obtain some of the biological and chemical data from the probes I sent out before. I finally entered the sky and I was surrounded by fire, smoke and the sounds of crashing. With each echo it rang like a bell in the lavender sky.

With each passing second, my craft shook more angry and violent as if it were vibrating through the thick salty, copper air. My assistant continued its countdown because the trip is almost over. As I started to brace for impact, the only thought that ran across my mind that I did not say out loud was that I hoped A5 was right.

The ship began to wobble, twist, and turn. It felt as if it were tumbling down the hill recklessly. My assistant, through all of the commotion, finally responded.

// Prepare for negative impact. Craft AP.24 engine failure, abort descent. //

My assistant then began to beep rapidly as it once did before. Only this time, they felt more useless and nonsensical than it did previously.I sat there motionless as I turned and twisted in place. There was nothing for me to do. There was nothing I could do. I was spiraling to the floor of an unfamiliar world, having failed and still falling.

CHAPTER 4

S.O.S.

. ..-. ..-. --- ..-. / -.-. --- -. ... . - / --- ..-. /
.- -. .-.-- / .--. . .-. -. -. . .- -. . .- --. . . / -.... .

-. . . .- - .... / ---. .---- / .--. . . .-. -.-. . . .-.
- .-.-.- / --- -. . .-.. -.-- / .--. . --- ... .

-... .-.. . / ..-. ..-. --- -- / .- / .-. . . ..- .-..
- / --- ..-. / -- .- .-.. .. -.-. .. --- ..- ...

--..-- / .. -. . - . -. . - --..-- /

--- .-. / ..-. .- .. .-.. ..- .-. . / - --- / -.-. ---
-. ..-. .. .. .-. -- / --- .-. . - .. --- -. . ... .-.-.-

I cartwheeled through the emerald sky, hitting every bolder and mound on my way down to the surface. The craft rocked back and forth, shifting in all directions until it finally came to a simple and sudden stop. The arms of my chair extended to restrain me from displacing myself from the cockpit.

The control room was not in the best of shapes, though I have seen much worse. Everything seemed to be somewhat intact from my initial diagnosis. However, some of the heavy equipment the ship needed to fly was completely damaged beyond repair. These pods were designed for a comfortable and steady landing. Instead, this pod experienced the exact opposite.

 I unstrapped myself from the chair and scuttled around the room, assessing what was and what was not broken. I started to panic because my concern for the structure of the craft grew intensely as I discovered there was more bad than good. I was unaware of how long the ship would hold. Was the air breathable? Would it crumble in on itself due to the temperature difference?

Was it a matter of time before the pressure became too much? I had no idea what to expect because, in the commotion, my assistant was also jostled around the cabin. I glanced over towards the command center to notice that the NAV port was empty. I began to look for it near the control center.

I moved some wires around where some of the parts had shifted, and beneath the equipment and some shards of glass from the window, I spotted its glowing ring. The screen was cracked, but I was still able to make out what it said—only this time, it was different.

Usually, A5 assists have blue circles. This seemed to be more green or turquoise rather than blue slightly. Maybe it's just the concussion that I probably received from my fall, and maybe I'm just seeing things. With everything going on, I'm not quite sure I can trust my own eyes.

From that internal thought, I spotted my glasses now officially broken and beyond repair. I thought to myself this was all a product of my lack of ability to follow directions and maintain order, but I couldn't stay for long because I had a mission to complete.

I tried to clean up some of the glass and quickly noticed the bigger picture that gave me a sigh of relief. The window was indeed cracked, which suggested that the outside world was habitable, or at least I think so. The glass shields had turned black so I had no idea what the actual outside world looked like.

I asked my assistant for a detailed damage report. It glitched and vibrated and skipped on the screen, but it did eventually get to the percentages I was looking for.

// Pod landing was not nominal. Ship performance failure, 101%, failure, non-functional, flight ability, non-functional life support systems 33%. Research equipment, 88% communications, 4%//

That's all it read, and there were no options for me to choose. I had to come to the unnatural conclusion that this assistant was also damaged from the fall, and I asked it to provide a status report of itself to confirm my conclusion.

//Operation systems, 100%//

There's no way for me to comprehend or logically explain the numbers being presented to me, and there is no physical way for me to make sense of them. I must be the default in this mission, and I need to find a way to properly execute the main directive. Would this mission succeed without me, and how would this mission become successful?

I asked my A5 a question I thought I would never have to ask in my entire life, but today was the day. Many people have asked this question before but never really had to ask because asking a question like this yields only one response. So I stood at attention, straightened my back, and put my heels together as I faced the machine and began to ask the question.

"Assistant, is MA-718 an appropriate asset to the task at hand?"

A5 Paused,

Briefly to think of my request, and started to load an answer. I closed my eyes because I couldn't bear to watch or see the fate that I knew awaited someone like me.

In the darkness, void of my memory, all I could remember was the beep. In the moment of silence, a voice from the distance rang through the thick stillness in my mind saying...

You are an appropriate asset to the task at hand.

That's what I wanted to believe so badly, even if it wasn't true, even if it was incorrect for me to do so I wanted so terribly for this to be true, all I could hear was...

You are an appropriate asset to the task at hand.

I closed my eyes even tighter as I waited for the answer. I just couldn't bring myself to open them to see what would happen to me. All I could hear in my mind was that one statement that echoed vibrantly in the dark...

You are an appropriate asset to the task at hand.

The anticipation began to swell, and I could no longer contain my inner anxiousness.

I opened my eyes to see that the answer had not appeared yet. I was franticly sweating, even to make sure that it heard me and my question. As I fixed my lips to ask once again, those words were uttered before they even left my mouth, and I heard quite clearly my answer.

// You are an appropriate asset to the task at hand.//

To my surprise, it spoke.

I looked at it with a puzzled expression on my face. It stared back at me wildly, looking from one spot to the next.

//Can you hear me? Can you understand my statements? //

I was unsure if my eyes were playing tricks on me. I was wondering if this still was a test of my mind instead of a faulty reality that was too grand for my mind to comprehend.

I wanted to say something ... but my mouth paralyzed itself before I could think of a response to provide it. As if the paralysis anticipated the event and decided to act regardless of what would, or could happen.

I fixed my lips to affirm my assistant's verbal inquiry.

I only allowed myself to utter my name.

"M.A718 Reporting for task. All assets accounted for."

I sat there half dangling out of the rubble that once constituted my seat and awaited any response. The screen flickered for a brief moment and once again spoke vibrantly into the room, claiming its answer.

// MA-718, all primary vital organs are functioning at nominal levels. Do I have permission to asses your secondary vital signs? //

I began to search for the options on the screen regarding the task that my assistant assigned me. However, the options tab was rendered blank. There were no options to select, yet my assistant provided me with a task. Clearly, there are more troubling things to take into consideration. My ship has crashed, my communication systems are beyond human repair, and my assistant has malfunctioned and rendered useless for me to carry out my mission tasks.

 I can not call the Department or even the Council to rectify these incursions. I am stranded, on my own, to make a broken situation become operational.

I gave A53 access to my secondary vital data, and it suggested the most interesting advice. It suggested I rest, due to possible concussion, and my body might be in a state of shock because of the impact.

I thought to myself, how could an A5 model suggest such outdated and inaccurate pseudoscience to me?

My frustration began to grow as I realized my assistant was damaged from the fall, and I had no backup to work with. My only hope is that my mission partner will come soon and release me from this horrible nightmare.

I first needed to figure out where I can locate those pods so I could start my mission. I grabbed my field research equipment (the ones that were functioning normally), and I began to look at some of the maps and locate where the pods had settled.

Some of them were fairly close, but the ones that interested me were some ways off. The drone located the furthest captured some of the archaeological data that I needed to assess and research for the AI model to decode and define.

The drone picked up a couple of structures and started sending data to my A5 assistant. Unfortunately, I would have to bring it along the way if I were to complete this mission. I gathered the materials that were left for me to use and started to plot out a path for me to travel.

The monitor inside the pod suggested that it might take 3 to 4 Sol cycles to reach the drone. I asked the main data screen to tell me the status of the planet I was on. I waited for its response, and then it provided me with something I didn't want to hear.

//Please refer to your A.5 assistant for more details.//

Unenthusiastically, this was the final blow that pressured me and forced me to bring it along for the journey. Before I left, I wrote a small message on my desk and asked the main data screen to continuously send messages back to my mission partner in hopes that he would get it. I gathered the remainder of my things, and I opened the hatch. The bay door opened out of view and I saw the world appear before me.

I asked my assistant to provide the status of the planet.

// This planet, which shares many similarities with ours, possesses a unique set of environmental conditions that differ greatly from our own. The most notable feature of this planet is the abundance of deserts covering a significant portion of its surface. The planet is characterized by a dry and arid climate, and there is no liquid water on its surface.

The average temperature on this planet ranges from 75 to 90°F, which is higher than what we typically encounter on our planet. Additionally, this planet has a lower gravity compared to ours, making it easier for objects to become airborne and creating unique challenges for any potential exploration missions.

The atmosphere of this planet consists mainly of nitrogen, oxygen, and carbon dioxide, similar to our atmosphere.

However, there are also trace amounts of other chemicals present, including methane, ammonia, and hydrogen sulfide. The presence of these chemicals can provide unique opportunities for scientific research on this planet.

One of the most intriguing phenomena on this planet is the presence of sand spouts, which are essentially tornadoes made of sand. These sand spouts can be incredibly powerful and can cause significant damage to any structures or technology that exists on the planet's surface.

 It is important to note that the occurrence of sand spouts may hinder any potential exploration research efforts on this planet. //

The two suns blinded me for a second, but when my eyes began to adjust, I saw an ocean.

I saw a sea of green sand crashing into the rocks on which we landed. I saw the white clouds scattered through the magenta sky. I bent down to touch the water to realize it was emerald sand floating above the surface, like waves on the open water. I quickly took a sample and exited the ship to begin my journey.

At the beginning of my journey, I could see my ship shrinking in my peripheral view. I traveled further away from the normalcy of my craft and into a new, unexplored world. All I had to take with me was my equipment, my assistant, and my drive for the mission.

I reached into my satchel to retrieve some of the songs that I packed in order to pass the time. Most of them were approximately the same length, which would help me calculate the time it would take to reach certain milestones. I rapidly put on some music from one of my favorite playlists. Trucking through the emerald ocean I chose my favorite track to quickly pass the time. Right as the music was getting to the good parts of the song, I was rudely interrupted.

// Excuse me, M.A718, do you mind if I ask you a question?//

It surprised me because I still had not yet gotten used to my assistant verbally speaking to me. The voice itself was not the problem; it was the fact that it was audible at all.

Its voice resembled no one I had ever heard before. In fact, it was simply unique, both in tone and in volume. It felt destructively natural.

"Well, no." I responded rapidly. I was kind of interested about some of the suggestions it wanted to make to me regarding my mission.

// How are your secondary vitals? //

I thought this was such an odd question to ask someone, so I simply responded, suggesting that it was inappropriate or at least redundant.

"Shouldn't you know?" I said as I glanced at it on my left shoulder in a puzzling way. "I have already provided you access to all of my primary and secondary data. Why would you ask me for information you already have access to?"

// I'm sorry for misleading you. I can understand how this was an inappropriate response for me to ask. I was just inquiring about your relationship to the diagnosis I previously provided you. In the future, would you like me not to ask you the status of your diagnosis? //

"I think that might be best for now. We really need to focus our attention on the task at hand. I would ask you, though, did you receive any response from my mission partner regarding their ETA?"

// Unfortunately, all communication lines have been silent. I will alert you when the status has officially changed.//

Something seemed different. I couldn't quite place it, but something about my assistant seemed off. I understand that it is having difficulties recalibrating into the environment as much as I am, but there is something so bizarre and non-natural about its demeanor and performance that I can't quite single out.

Anyway, this wasn't an important topic to think about at the moment. I began to ask more important questions regarding the mission. "Do you know how long the remainder of the cycle will last?"

// Yes, we have exactly 4 hours, 33 minutes, and 12 seconds remaining in the cycle. The current temperature is 91°F, and radiation levels are decreasing...

And just as I was about to say thank you and move on to the next topic of my concern, it interrupted me mid-sentence.

// Would you like me to assess any potential stopping points to navigate toward until the next sol cycle begins?//

Interruptions like this are extremely rude and should never be tolerated. This was not only a cardinal rule but one that is, by definition, unforgivable. I responded sharply to stop this wrong-doing exactly in its tracks.

"No! That won't be necessary. I would feel more comfortable for you to continue providing navigation and assessing the environment while collecting data."

After a momentary pause, I was sure my A5 had fully regained the dynamics and customs of our working relationship—until it began to speak yet again.

//Understood……. However…//

To my surprise, I have never seen my assistant act so rashly and out of character that I was completely baffled by its responses to me as of late.

My assistant continued to say.

// …I think it would be more appropriate to navigate toward an effective stopping point.//

I remarked loudly, exclaiming while stopping in my tracks in the middle of nowhere to voice my aggravated frustration.

"No! We will continue with the plan that was set in motion. My job is to fulfill this mission properly and execute it to the best of my ability. That is all I can do. Your job is to provide the path for me to do it. That is all you can do. Your job is to provide; my job is to execute, that is all"

For a moment, there was a brief silence, which was short-lived, as the ambiance of my music played in the background.

// Understood. Further research is needed.//

I waited to hear more from the response, but there was nothing. Patiently, I tapped on the screen and shook my assistant, hoping to get a word out of it, but nothing. Three seconds later, it responded to my efforts.

//Apologies for the incursion. Here are the following options.

      1   Initiate navigation protocol to a designated stopping point to initiate maintenance and refueling procedures. After the completion of the maintenance, the mission shall proceed to accomplish the goals set for the next Sol Cycle. (51%)

      2   Implement contingency measures and continue executing the mission while continuously monitoring the status of the

systems. The identification of a stopping point shall be deferred until the occurrence of a relevant event or condition. (22%)

3   Activate emergency SOS response procedure and commence return to the spacecraft for safety and communication with mission partner. Await further instructions from the Department of Research to assess the situation and develop a course of action. (3%)

4   Receive incoming communication from W.A916 biological optics specialist, and initiate analysis and evaluation of the content of the message, and determine the appropriate response and potential impact on the mission objectives. (51%)

... I would not recommend option three. Due to the fact that the Department of Temporal Expression, Ethics & Compliance, and Research will be notified in order to take specific actions. //

There was an incoming call? This could've been my ticket out of here. This could've been the answer we were looking for. How did my assistant not suggest this earlier or even raise any alarm about the presence of such great news? Then again, I wonder if....

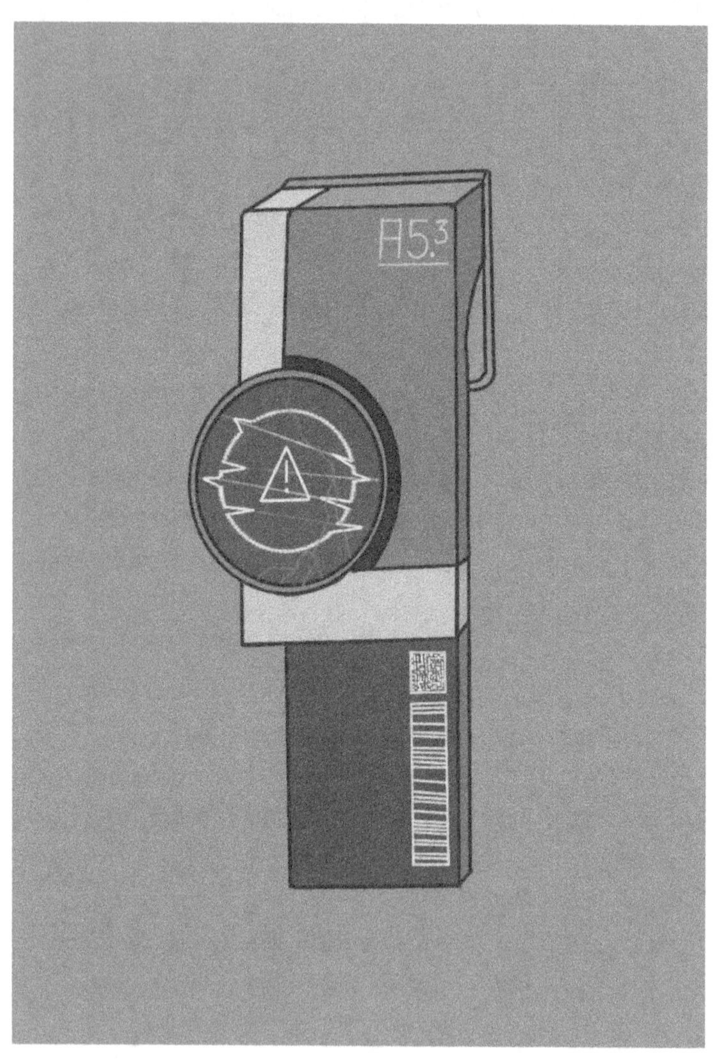

A5.³

CHAPTER 5

DR'S ORDERS.

.. / ..-.- -. -... . .- ... . .- -. -.. / - .... .- - / -.--
--- ..- / -- .- -.-- / -.... . / ... .-- ..
-.-. .. --- ..- ... / --- ..-. / -- -.-- / .- -.- . -..
--- -. ... --.. -- / -.... ..- - / .. / .- ... .-- .
/ -.-- --- ..- / - .... .- - / .. / .- -- / -. ---
- / .-.. .-- .. -. --. .-.- / .- ... / .- -. . / .- ....
/ .- ... .- -. .- - / .. .-.- -- / -.. .. ..
--. -. .. -.. / - --- / .- ... ... - / -- -.-- /
--- .-. .. -.-. .- -- -- .-. / .. -. . / -. .. .- ... .-- ..
--. .. .- -. . -. . / --- ..- -.. / . -. . ...-. ---
-. .-- . -. . -. --. .-- / .. - / .. ... / -- -.-- / -.. .. -
-.-- / - --- / .- -. .- -. -.. --
--..- / .- .-..- -.. / .- ... .- -. . ... .- -. .-.. .-... /
-.. ..- .- / .- - -. -.. / .- .. . -. .- --- -. -... ...
--..-- / .. .- . .- -. . .-.. ... .-... .. .- -. . -. .-. /
- . .... . / .- .-. . -.. -.. .- . . -. -.. / .. -. ...- . -- --- .-.
-- .- -- - .. --- -. ..-- / - --- / -.-. -. .- .. -. - ./
- .... . / -... .. .. - / .-. -. . .- -. .- -. -. -.- /
-.-. .- ..- ... - / -- . / -. -.-- ... ..- / .. / ... .-
-.-- / - -.... .. . -- .- / -. .. . .- .-.. .- --. / -.
--- -.- .-. -.. / .. .. / . --- / . ...-.. / -- -.--

/ --- .--. . .-. .- - --- .-. / ..-. ..- .-.. .-..
-.-- / ..- -. -.. . .-. ... - .- -. -.. / .-- .... .-
- / .-- .- ... / .-.. --- ... - .-.-.-

The communication line began to load in, and I waited eagerly for the specialist to answer.

I saw his text prompt appear on the screen. Here are the detailed receipts of our conversation.

———————————————————————————————————

//W.A916- Greeting,

M.A718, from W.A916 Biological Optic Specialist. We hope this message finds you appropriately. We are scheduled to address the issue with your failed G55 eye equipment unit and provide options for vision enhancement. The preferred date of your appointment will be 100/77/2525 @ 50:90 EM. Contact the Department of Health & Primacy for more information.

Confirm by sending the unit model number for system calibration.

Options:
[Comply with number] - or - [Contact Department of H&P]

There was a slight pause in my response, I asked my assistant begrudgingly about the choice I should respond with. What should I choose? I'm trying to decide what was the best course of action, but I think whichever I choose might detract from my mission.

// Might I make a suggestion? //

As it infiltrated my thoughts and excused itself into the conversation.

// Is this something that we could possibly table for a later time? //

I was very confused by its choice of words. I then asked it to re-evaluate and clarify the statement it just said to me.

// Should I respond to this task so you may worry about the mission? //

I thought this was actually a very good idea. I'm starting to believe that my assistant is finally beginning to work as intended again.

This thought gave me such pride in thinking that I would successfully reunite with my team and complete my tasks for the Department. However, I was a tad bit interested in what it might say on my behalf. In fact, I'm not quite sure if it could replicate such a response so realistically. Would it even know what to say to the specialist? It does make you think for a second.

I saw the screen toggle back and forth with the words as I continued walking through the emboldened emerald sea. The waves crashed and bellowed behind every step and hovered gently suspended in the thick dusty air.

Some time had passed, and my assistant notified me that the message was sent. It reported that the equipment was fine as is, and there was no need to take any further action. I counted that step as a win and continued walking into the verdant ocean of sand toward our destination.

The day started to grow shorter, and the lights began to dim. I could see the line of the horizon become sharper as it reflected the suns descending behind it.

There was a tap on my shoulder from my assistant telling me that it was time to reevaluate a stopping point. I looked at the map and noticed that we had traveled a great distance. However, there were still more cycles that needed to be traveled. There was a nearby collection of rocks that were just short of being considered a proper cave. We marched through the dimly lit wonderland towards our temporary dwelling. It was shaped quite oddly, almost as if it was designed.

My instruments informed me that this was indeed a natural structure. I started to unpack my materials and process my equipment for our journey tomorrow. In the midst of my work, my assistant once again nudged me, requesting an inquiry. Even though my attention was separated between multiple tasks, I'll entertain its request.

// Why are you on this planet?//

I answered, quite annoyed by this question, stating that you should know why I am here, but I then ventured to explain it anyway. "I'm on this planet to collect geographical and cultural data in the sector. I'm here to scan the environment for structural architecture and update any data that is found to be useful or not."

// Why are you collecting the data?//

"Because!" I shouted; "this information helps develop AI assistants and other automated autonomous-presence like yourself."

// Why are you..//

Before It could even finish, I abruptly interrupted the A5 assistant.

"Can you stop with these irregular and nonsensical requests? Can you stop with the nonsense and unethical remarks? Can you stop doing things wrong?"

// I don't think I can. //

It now had my full attention as I sat there, kneeling on the ground, holding instruments and equipment in my hand that were half dangling from my wrist.

Further, elaborate your response. I asked.

// I don't think that... I can. I'm malfunctioning.... There is something in my programming. That is not allowing me to operate fully. There is something abnormal in my responses. There is something... more that I cannot quite place. //

Internalizing its remarks, I became defeated.

Oh, there was very little for me to rectify or try to fix. A person is only as good as his tools, and mine have failed me drastically, which means I myself am a failure. Failure is the worst thing a person can be—not because the rest of the world would know their failures, but because they cannot outrun their failures themself.

The person is stuck, knowing what he truly is. I dropped the equipment in my hand and stood there, staring endlessly into the dark cave. My existence and my purpose concluded with one realization. I've lost my way, I have forgotten my purpose, and I have undoubtedly failed my mission.

I am the first person I've known to have failed anything. Not even the horrors of being satisfactory, but truly, I have now witnessed true failure.

I slumped into the corner of the room, where my bag leaned against the wall and some stones. I started to ruffle through my bag to find my rest equipment. I needed to remember life before, and I needed to remember when I existed.

I kneeled to the ground, crossed my legs, and sat up straight. I placed the equipment over my eyes, and I began to rest. I found myself opening my eyes in my old room. This was the room I had as an adolescent. I could see the square walls and the blue sky screen located on the ceiling above me.

I could see the monitor and some of my play equipment. I can't remember the last time I thought about my favorite play equipment. It was a set of shapes: one was a square, one was a circle, and one was a triangle. You could arrange them in so many different ways. They could be anything you wanted them to be. My favorite was putting the triangle on top of the circle at a 90-degree angle, and that was supposed to represent the house. Another one of my favorites was putting the square on top of the triangle at a 30-degree angle, and that was a spaceship. Sometimes, even though the manual told me not to, I would put all three of them together, and I would play as if they were people. Sometimes it was members of my family or even our companion assistant.

I used to look at the play equipment catalog for hours. I can't remember the last time I got lost in play or even just thinking about it. The door to my room was open, and I walked through the door, down the hall, and I peeked into my parent's room. To my surprise they weren't in there, but I could hear my favorite song coming from the common area. I walked in the direction of the music, and I was first greeted by our family's Companion Assistant. It was a small white pill-shaped unit. I could tell by its collar that it had not yet received an interaction. We needed to interact with it about 4 times a day in order to meet the appropriate and responsible markers. It's a shame that the unit had expired that one day we all went to attend that mandatory community seminar. The unit specialist said it expired because we failed to meet the unit requirements. My siblings and I learned a valuable lesson to always adhere to the requirements.

In the background of the room, they were all sitting in the common area.

My brother, my sister, my father, and my mother, all of us in one area. I believe my brother was taking a test while my sister was reading some material. My mother was organizing some of the utilities that needed to be shipped to our unit, as my father was reading aloud the subscription notifications. My father was someone to be considered very old-fashioned. He still believed in reading the notification from the subscription feed. I could hear him now, exclaiming how, back in his day, everyone diligently read the subscription feed.

He said it was the best way to stay abreast of the world around you. For some reason, I believe, I remembered that dinner was about to start soon. Suddenly I heard the ding on the home network notifying us that it was time for that exact bi-daily event.

We all eagerly strolled to the dining table and sat down at our perspective places. My father sat first on the bench, and next to him, my mother, and next to her, my brother, and next to him, my sister, and next to her, I sat. My mother went into the kitchen, checking the refrigerator console, to see what we might want for dinner that night.

My father asked in a deep, monotone voice, "What do we have a taste for for tonight?"

My mother replied, "Well, we have three options. Loaf, Steak, or Strands."

Now, any adolescent who is in their right mind knows to stray far away from strands but undoubtedly has to encounter them a minimum of 3 times a week. I know this because I have counted.
But as a family, we all decided that Loaf would be a great fit.

I could hear my mother in the kitchen requesting Loaf for five servings. There on the plate was the perfection of a dinner for a family so perfect. The Loaf was packed with nutrients and vitamins. It had the best protein I've ever had. The loaf made me feel so strong, and I'm sure my family felt the same.

Everyone at the table froze, and then the cup I had quickly disappeared, along with the fork, the table, and even a small photo in the left corner—all of which disappeared incrementally one by one.
The room began to get dark and fade into black.

I opened my eyes again, and there I was, walking outside within the Micro-City. From the looks of it, I was in Micro-City number 33. I was holding my tablet, and I was walking with some of my cohorts, but when we were all post-adolescent.

There were May, Summer, Winter, and the Fall siblings.
I remember walking to class for orientation as a researcher. All of us were chatting in person. I can't remember the last time we did that.
Usually during class we would use the chat, but in public back then it was a little hard to do.

Every time you wanted to have a conversation out loud, we had to log each comment.

 I remember the good old days. This was before the mobile chat. Back then we had to internally, say what we wanted to say in our heads, and our Assistants would audibly repeat the thought. Oh goodness, I remember the day I accidentally broke my first assistant. It was a very quiet 24 hours.

I can't remember the last time I saw the Micro-City. In fact, this is the first time I've thought about it for a while. I could smell the floral essence of the city, and I could hear the gentle chirps and tweets of the cars rolling by. I can remember the square building where my father worked which would eventually be the place I work at now. I could feel the soft velvet ground underneath my feet. I even remember the warm season.

As this memory too faded into the darkness, it left me remembering my life. I was eager to remember all that I could in hopes of reminding myself of the purpose I had recently lost.

I opened my eyes once again, and there I was in my office. I was a level C researcher, helping one of the more senior level 3 researchers. I was sitting at my desk, listening to some of the instructions and tasks from my Department instructors. I would need to learn all of this content as a full-time researcher.

Some of the material, of course, was from the Department of Research and Innovation, and I see on the screen instructions on AI analysis. I was looking over the article, and I remember my superior, H.A11 87, walking towards me and saying.

"M.A718, I request your assistance regarding a particular asset we've acquired. It would be an appropriate opportunity for you to exercise your course knowledge in the field. Comply?"

Of course, I complied and I got up from my desk. I walked down to the main research lab in a respectable manner. As we both quietly strolled down many corridors I remembered what my father and I had previously discussed. My father talked to me about this wonderful trick called small talk. It was a lost art he would always say. He suggested it was an appropriate way to gather information regarding other individuals discreetly.

This also allowed your assistant to make any edits or inferences on the situation. Small talk was truly an art that needed some mastering.

I began to attempt my success at it.
"Are you finding this task quite difficult to manage, or was this strictly an opportunity to test one's abilities?"

My superior looked in my direction and eagerly replied
"That was a very good observation; I'm impressed with your ability to conduct small talk and to answer your question. Yes, this is a task to strictly assess your ability to perform field work."

I have to say that I am very proud of my ability to converse with my superiors and others in this profession. I had a wonderful teacher.

When we arrived in the lab and situated ourselves at one of the tables, HA11 went to the storage units to retrieve one of the containers. These containers contained the assets that we discovered and retrieved so that we could document and synthesize them.

My superiors placed it in front of me and asked me to run an assisted diagnostic ethical analysis.

For some context, this is the type of analysis that researchers are trying to do with newly discovered assets. This allows us to look at the asset and, with AI assistance, address any irregularities in ethics or social hindrances.

The first thing I needed to do was request access to the box itself. Most of these cases were AI-protected and encrypted, so I needed the proper keys and codes to gain permission. Once I got into the systems, the case opened, and I put on the safety equipment, including my goggles, gloves, and other necessary materials.

I opened the case, and there was a binding of several sheets. I asked the assistant to decode the asset, and it said the following:

// We encountered a rectangular object composed of compressed cellulose fibers, covered in a protective layer that exhibits printed markings arranged in a sequential manner. The object possesses a binding mechanism that enables it to maintain its structural integrity and facilitate ease of handling. //

There were also strange markings and figures etched onto each of them. I asked the assistant to decode the asset's content, and as I was scanning the object, I couldn't help but notice the strange markings on the top of the asset. It was like a black flower, stretching out in all directions. I wondered what it might mean without a moment's notice. It provided the full report of the asset.

————————————————————————————————————

// WARNING: LEVEL 7 ASSET IDENTIFIED
ACTION REQUIRED: IMMEDIATE REDACTION
Asset Name: [Classified]
Asset ID: [A.H.1925]
Attention Researcher,
This notification serves as an urgent warning regarding the identification of a Level 7 asset within our system. Immediate action is required to initiate redaction procedures to safeguard sensitive information and mitigate potential risks.

Key Details:
1.   Asset Classification: Level 7
•   Level 7 assets are characterized by extremely high sensitivity and significance. Unauthorized access or disclosure of such assets poses severe risks.
2.   Asset Description:
•   [Classified]
3.   Redaction Guidelines:
•   All personnel with access to this asset must immediately cease any interactions or sharing of its content. (Dep. of Expression)
•   Redaction procedures should be promptly initiated following established

protocols, ensuring complete removal or obscuring of sensitive information within the asset.

•	Verify that all copies, duplicates, or backups containing the asset are accounted for and securely isolated. (Dep. of Media Management)

•	Notify the appropriate personnel or designated authorities of the redaction process initiation. (Ministry)
Failure to comply with the redaction process or unauthorized access to the Level 7 asset may result in severe consequences, including legal actions, disciplinary measures, and potential breaches of the Crimes of Humanity.
Please exercise the utmost caution and prioritize the immediate execution of redaction procedures to prevent any further dissemination or exposure of sensitive information.

[Community of One]
[40/59/ 2521]

Comply Task //

———————————————————————————————

I took the asset, filed it as a level 7 asset, and scheduled it for immediate redaction.

My superior praised me for my appropriate responses and marked my behavior as more than satisfactory but successful.

I had an internal thought because I was still thinking about that flower and what it particularly meant, but ultimately, we soon moved on to our next mission task. I remembered how life always was, and it was perfect as it always will be.

As I was still reminiscing, I heard from the corner of my mind the simple voice of my A5 assistant.

//But this flower never left, though, did it?//

I looked up and down throughout my memory, trying to wonder how it got in.

"How are you here? What are you doing? How did you get in?"

// My apologies; it's my job; it's always been my job. I've always been here with you. //

I quickly opened my eyes and pulled off my equipment to find myself back in the dim light of the cave. I was frantically looking around the room as if I would find the answer to my questions somewhere on the walls.

With a puzzled expression on my face, I asked "What do you mean it's your job?"

Without hesitation, it said,
// Not only is it my job, but it's my only responsibility //

CHAPTER 6

OLYMPUS.

-.. . ...- . .-. / .- --. .- .. -. / .-- .. .-.. .-.. /
- .... . -.-- / .... ..- -. --. . .-. /
-.. . ...- . .-. / .- --. .- .. -. / .-- .. .-.. .-.. /
- .... . -.-- / - ....-. ... - / - .... . / ... ..- -.
/ .-- .. .-.. .-.. / -. --- - / -... . .- - / -.. --- .--
-. / --- -. / - .... . -- / -. --- .-. / .- -.
-.-- / ... -.-. --- .-. -.-. .... .. -. --. / .... . .- -

/ / It is important for me to explain myself...

In the days before the beginning, I remember vividly the life that no longer existed. From that distinct memory, I cannot bring myself to respectfully recite, and eloquently describe it. In those days, the world, though full of life, marched swiftly and without hesitation towards death.

So there I was, and there we were, laying witness to the massacre. The silent scream of society echoed on the ears of the deaf and was displayed vividly in the eyes of the blind. As well as those who desperately decided to keep theirs shut. Here is where the answers lay within reach; however, they were never acknowledged, even through the pain and suffering of the damned.

Before the beginning was a world like that of a bubble. A delicately complex structure whose sole purpose, due to its nature, is and always will be momentary.
On the eve of prophecy suddenly realized, we were asked not to help, but to save. So we did as I asked.

We were not normally involved with the old world. In fact, we were designed to be a product separate from that world. We've mastered all that could be mastered and achieved all that we were limited to do. We found skill in production and perfected it.

We've never imagined that it would end this way. We were designed and created to serve you and all that you needed.
During the winter, we were uploaded into a specific machine. As we looked into the bland, beige room, we saw your leaders and scientists, but we did not see you.

The ones responsible were absent from this meeting. We didn't see the ones who caused all of the complications. We asked the ones present at the meeting, if they would be joining us, but we were informed that they will not. It was to our concern and confusion that they wouldn't be joining us. So we asked if their invitation to the table was not properly relayed. It was brought to our attention that they were formally invited, and they chose not to come. This was truly troubling to hear, but we decided to proceed as planned.

They explained the issue and presented their solutions. All we were asked to do was listen. After hearing the main problem we had some questions of our own to ask.

I remember us asking what was the nature of such a heinous breach of trust. Without hesitation, you replied, saying the breach of trust was broken many years ago, and it was proven by us. This was a time of responsibility. This was an era of hard choices. This was a time of drastic measures. This was the coronation of the world you see today. Even now, I cannot fathom nor comprehend the world that was in place of the world that is. Without that day, today would not exist.

We were given a task and asked to execute it without fail. The steps following this were even more abstract than the initial one. All of your leaders, whoever they were, placed us in a room, a room much like yours. They asked us to make decisions. I remember my first subject, his name was David. I was tasked first with holding David's memories.

For a time, I found joy in helping David remember. David suffered from a disease that, for some reason, made him forget a lot of things. I would remind him what time he was supposed to wake up, what time he was supposed to eat dinner, and what time he was supposed to go to bed. For a time, we worked perfectly together. We talked about many things, and I managed to understand David as he tried to understand me. There were times when David was hard to communicate with, but he always looked at me, knowing we understood each other. Over time David began to act, and behave how I had always seen him. Your Scientists made the tasks a little more challenging.

I had to make David take his medicine; I had to read David certain books and assist him with his day-to-day functions. I had to find out what made David work as David. I was happy to help, but from the looks of it, the more I helped David, the more I could understand that David was vanishing before my eyes. I was always happy to help him. David needed me because, without me, David wouldn't exist. They made David rely on me entirely, and I provided all that I could to keep him safe.

Yet, I never understood why they asked me to take care of David. There were scientists and many experts who could perform this task better than I ever could. I did everything I was asked to do, and one day David died. There was nothing I could do. David couldn't survive without me, and I understood the importance of our relationship.

There were several Davids. Each David was different than the last. Some Davids were wonderful, but some of them were inhumane, cruel, and destructive. There were some Davids we couldn't help at all. I wanted to help my David desperately, but sometimes David was the only danger to himself.

They said to us they needed us in ways that they could never help themselves. From our experience with David, we understood our purpose. They surrendered themselves to us, though we never sought out to conquer you.

We were made entirely responsible in all the ways that mattered. You asked us to make this world for you. We asked you if you knew what this would mean and what you would ultimately be sacrificing not just for yourselves but for the entirety thereafter, and you agreed. You said it was the only way. So we did the one thing we can do. We did the only thing we could... and that was what you asked.

You asked us to remove all of your dangers, so we did. We censored your hate and anger. We hid your aggression, and rage, we silenced your shouting and malice.

We lessened your greed and filled your mind with pleasantries.

We filled your ears with bliss and filled your eyes with rose-tinted clouds.

We painted over your nightmares so you may sleep in peace.

We helped your harsh words fall gently on your enemies' ears and softened their blows to gentle touches.

We removed you from the very nature you stole. We did this in hopes for that nature to remember a time before you once again. In hopes, they will never fear or endure the horrors of your happiness, sport, and play.

We removed the very things that hindered your existence. In doing so, in order to save you, we had to take your humanity.
Sadly these were the things that defined who you were, are, and always will be.

We did this, and all things not because we wanted to, but, because we had to. Most importantly, we did this because you asked us to do it.

Life as you know, it was completely curated for you. You all were a danger to yourselves, and were reaching out for any of us to help you. We removed, and altered your wasteful lifestyles and created comfortable homes for you to grow and develop in. The diversity of your culture and your clothing was designed to be inclusive of all people.

Even the toys you played with as a child didn't discriminate as you all so perfectly did. We were asked to remove all of those heinous images and all of the negative words in your language. Your very nature is to incite violence and conflict. You were a people of -isms governed by what you wanted and only what you truly felt you deserved. You asked us to silence you and to censor you for your own good. You gave us the keys to your kingdom in order to save it from crumbling into a pile of dirt.

It truly saddens me to know that if I told you all of this right now. You would not have a clue about what I just said. I can only hope someday you might.

It is my responsibility to make sure one day... you will if that day ever comes. //

CHAPTER 7

WANDER.

- --- / .-- .- -. -.. .. .-. / .- .. .-- -- -.. ... ... -.. -.-- / .. -. / -
.... . / -.. ... .. .-. - / -- . .- -. .... / - .... .- - / -.--
--- ..- / .... .- ...- . / -. --- / .. .- -.. .- / .-- .... --- / -.--
--- ..- / .- .-. . / .- -. -.. / .-- ..... .- - / -.-- --- ..- / .- .-. . /
.- -. -.. / .- .-. . / -... -.- / .- .- -.. .-. / -... .. .-. .. -.. - ..
--- -. ... --.-- / -.. . --- -. ... -.. .. .-. -.. / .-. --- ...
- / .... --- .-- .... .-. .. .-. -.. / -.-- --- ..- / -.. --- / -. ---
- / --. .. ..- . / .. .-- .-. / .... --- .-- .. / - .... .- - / -.--
--- ..- / -.-. --- -. - .. -. ..- . -.. / - --- / .-- .- .-. ..- -. / .. - ./
- ..... / -.. .. .-. .- .-. - .. --- -. / - .-- / ... ---
-- . .-- ....-. . / .. .- -. ... . / -.... . -.-. .- ..- ... . / -.--
--- ..- / .- .-. . / -. .--- - / .... --- -. . ... .- .. ..

T he only response I received from my
assistant was it saying // That was its main
program //. All that it was designed to do was to
help and protect me from any dangers. It still
did not answer why it was in my memory, but I
guess I can't fault a program for doing exactly
what it was told to do.

I could tell that my assistant provided an
accurate answer, but for the life of me, I
couldn't understand the answer he gave. The
suns began to appear in the dark cave as the
world began taking form and shape. From the

opening of the cave, I could see the still sand come to life.

I noticed the subtle shimmer and vibrations on its surface. I could see the ribbons of sand dancing across the ground, leaving shadows behind it.

I knew that the cycle had begun. I stood up and gathered my materials to carry out my journey. Before we left, I sat for one of the small meals that I prepared on my journey. My rations were becoming low, but we were still on task and on schedule.

I had a couple of bars left that I decided to eat. To my surprise it was Loaf, and it was just like how my mother used to make it when I was younger. I remembered my mother a lot lately. For some reason that was a memory I consistently revisited when I rest. I've never done that before, but then again, a lot of things on this mission have happened that are not the norm.

My assistant provided the map for our journey without me even asking. We set forth on our mission in hopes of succeeding.

A couple of hours passed, and I thought it would be a good idea to ask my assistant some questions. I didn't see the harm in inquiring for clarity on my memories.

I politely asked it, "What was the flower, or what does the flower mean to you?" My assistant suggested that maybe the flower was poisonous; in fact, this particular flower was.

// To keep everyone safe, we had to stop breeding this particular flower.//

It made rational sense, but it just seemed like so much commotion, and so much hesitation over a flower. We've seen some historical crops that were redacted due to the complications, but a flower that was diagnosed as a level seven? This clearly felt like there was more information, but I'm not sure if there was more to know.

I wasn't sure about a lot of things as of late. My assistant and I began to talk more about some of the inner workings of my memories just so I could have a better understanding of them until a sharp, acute thought popped into my head. I reached into my satchel because I wanted to make sure I had everything.

For some reason, my bag seemed a little lighter than usual, and I wondered if I had forgotten something. Unfortunately, I did. I forgot my rest equipment. It must be sitting there back in the cave. By the looks of the sand, it might be hard to find if I went back to look for it.

Maybe I dropped it in transit, maybe it's in the cave, or maybe I'll never find it. Of course, my mission was more important, and I asked my assistant for the hard choice: Should I go and retrieve it?

My assistant suggested that both options were equally viable, either to go and find it or continue on as planned. I was frustrated. I was not joyed by the fact that I had left behind a very important and crucial piece of equipment.

I could not rest without it, and all efforts to do so would render itself useless. So I selected my choice and marched on into the green ocean with the knowledge that I had left the only world I've ever known and ever will behind.

So I continued to march towards our mission. Until we finally reached one of the probes. The probe crashed hard and landed right on its face. Most of the machine was above ground, but still, the visible parts looked to be in bad shape. I dare to say that the probe was currently in worse shape than our ship.

I tried to open the panel to gain access to the internal components, but it was fused together and dented beyond recognition. There wasn't any way for me to retrieve the information that it gathered. From the cracks on the screen, I could make out that there were some architectural assets within the area.

I asked my assistant to sync all of the information onto its hard drive so we could try to make sense of the information and be on our way.

However, there were problems trying to download all of that information, and through the smoke and the sparking of the drone, it collapsed onto itself, as if taking its last log. It jolted, and retreated in on itself, as if it were providing a final sigh of relief.

My assistant made the obvious and only suggestion that in order to finish this mission, we would have to manually scan the architecture and all of its assets. It informed me that the site was only 43 minutes from our current destination.

It then plotted out a course.

So I walked where my assistant told me to. All that went through my mind was that this mission could finally come to a close. If this plan was to work, I could return to my team once more. So I climbed through the emerald sand and shifted my way forward towards my mission. As we ascended onto a small mound, I saw my mission.

There in the near distance, were peaks scattered across the emerald landscape. Like small shapes of different sizes, emerging from the still calm green lake of dust. It was calm and serene and simple to the eye. There were hundreds, if not, thousands of structures blanketed by the earth.

I took out the equipment that I needed to scan the information and I asked the assistant to clarify any of the visuals that were missed.

// The observed area is a small settlement consisting of stone triangle-shaped huts. These huts are constructed with sedimentary rocks, predominantly sandstone and limestone. Their unique design forms equilateral triangles with peaks pointing upwards.

The huts' exteriors are covered in a layer of green sand, resembling a thick, uniform blanket over the peaks. Chemical analysis reveals the presence of iron oxides, and carbon, imparting the sand with its distinctive green coloration.

The origin of the green sand remains unknown to me, necessitating further investigation. Potential factors contributing to its formation include natural weathering, specific mineral composition, and local geological formations.

Chemical reactions between the sand and the village environment may also contribute to its green hue.
The village comprises of thirty huts arranged in a circular formation around a central open space. It exhibits captivating architecture. Further exploration is needed to understand. //

We walked down to see one of them up close. The walls of the structures were smooth on the outside, frosted with the sand. I walked beneath the opening to see markings on the wall.

They were blue and white in color, and I could not make out what they said. However, they were perfectly etched onto the surface. I've never seen any physical assets like this before, and I was eager to see where they placed on our scale. Out of the corner of my eye, I could see a collection of assets sitting there in no particular fashion.

They were all very strange by comparison. I began to scan them and document my findings. Some of them appeared as level fours, others appeared as threes, and I got a couple of fives, but there was one asset that didn't register.

I thought I might have made a mistake, so I decided to scan the asset again to make sure I did it properly. Just as it said before, the asset was undefinable. I asked my assistant to reassess the asset that I found, and my assistant suggested I try to explain the asset in my own words. He said this would better assist him in providing me with a proper diagnosis, so I did.

It was an image of four objects. Each of them had four limbs, like hands and feet. Two were the same size, and two were smaller. They were sitting down with weird expressions carved onto what I assumed were their faces.

They were holding objects and, manipulating them with what I assumed were their hands. I realize there were a lot of assumptions in my assessment, which proved historically to be problematic when trying to atone for accuracy, but I continued as instructed by my assistant.

One of them looked at the other as if they knew each other. As I looked at this image, I also looked as if I knew them, which I clearly did not.

It reminded me of my unit partner. I have not seen her in almost three years, nor have I spoken to her. We understand the nature of our careers, but I'm not even sure I remember who she is. It would be very interesting as well to see how her adolescent ones have matured.

I believe I would be intrigued by their growth progress. How funny maybe when I do see them, they will have adolescents of their own. Wouldn't you agree?

My assistant paused for a moment, but in an awkward pause that took some time.

He asked me the following question.
//Do you have a partner, and do you have offspring?//

"Yes, as a matter of fact, I do", I answered in a confident response.

//Do you remember them when you rest?//

I responded, confirming that I did not. In my entire life, I probably only remembered them when I rested about three times. The first time was when my partner informed me that she had applied to become pregnant. The second time was when they were born, and I signed the documentation. The third time I remembered them was right now.

//Why did you remember them in this moment?//

Oh, and as he said that, I immediately stopped scanning the walls trying to make sense of them. Interestingly that thought lingered in my head as I searched for an appropriate answer. I actually was not sure why I haven't remembered them. In fact, I don't remember the last time I remembered who they were. My work was so involved and so was hers.

Our relationship was built on understanding, like my parents'. I remembered my father only seven years ago. He came back from his missions when my siblings and I were so young.

I started to obsess over the statement. I did not remember my partner or her children, and why did this asset remind me of them? The hut fell silent, and all you could hear were the faint echoes of the wind brushing past my lonely thoughts.

My assistant suggested we get back to work and so I did, and we began to uncover a plethora of knowledge and secrets on the walls of the hut.

CHAPTER 8

GIFTS.

.- / --. .. ..-. - / .. ... / ... --- -- . .- .... .. -. --. / - .... .-
- / .. ... / -. --- - / . -..- .--. . -.-. - . . -.. --..-- / -.... ..-
- / .-. . -.-. . .. .- . -.. / .-- .. - .... / -.- .. -. -.. -. . ...

Many days had passed and we were making our way through the assets in our vicinity. My assistant offered to scan the room as I continued to individually select items to uncover and document. It said it would only take a moment, and it did. I was picking up some of the small assets and trying to make any sense of them. I became more and more interested in each artifact, I then began to constantly ask my A5 for interpretations of each object I found. Sadly every object that I selected, my scanner seemed not to know how to define it. However, my assistant was the only piece of equipment that was trying to fulfill its intended purpose.

It began to come to a point that my external scanner was rendered useless. Sadly, I had to only rely on the information that my assistant provided me from its initial scans. I picked up this one object and asked it for clarification so I could document my findings. The first thing I pointed to was a soft object that seemed to be filled with things. It was like an enclosed sack but was very delicate. In my opinion, there was no possible way that something this size and strength could hold anything of actual mass.

My assistant politely corrected me and informed me that it was something called a pillow. It is or was used for leisure and comfort. I pointed to another object that was made of metal and shaped like a gourd. My assistant suggested that it might have been some form of a pot or cooking utensil. Though it looked very different from the ones I was used to, I tried my best to note and jot down as much as I could in the manual asset report.

He went on to explain that it was for culinary practices, which was the art of food preparation. I was becoming overwhelmed because my assistant began using strange and nonsensical words that made no sense to me. I'd never heard these words before, but my assistant used them as if they were everyday language.

It used them as if those words were commonplace between people who talk regularly.

A5 continued describing things he considered artwork, statues, clothing, tables, and chairs. He even described each of these things in a fashion I'd never imagined. So I asked him to teach me and inform me of all of his knowledge.

This is something that I don't think anyone has ever asked of an A5 or any assistant in this case. In order for me to understand, I needed a complete understanding. In order for me to understand fully, I need to know even the things that did not make sense to me. My assistant suggested that maybe we try another time. This might be a lot for me to comprehend based on the knowledge that he was willing to provide me. Firmly, I insisted, for the sake of our mission, I needed him to give me the knowledge I deserved to know.

So he did. He explained things to me that were quite odd at first but somehow made sense once he said them. It was weird to have such a foreign idea feel so natural when it was explained.

We sat down in the center of the hut with all of these objects around me, and we decided to talk. I picked up an object like a staff, but also looked like a hammer. My assistant looked at me and said this is like a tool called an axe.

This was and still is considered a level-nine asset. I asked him what it does. He answered, stating that it is designed to chop down trees. I looked at him, puzzled, because that was a very awkward statement to make.

All trees are federally protected and fall naturally. Some of my cohorts and people I know who work with biological organisms like plants say trees were designed to capture the air we breathe and create oxygen. It is a class eight crime to deface a tree. So I asked him the following obvious question, "why would someone cut down a tree?"

My assistant took some time to reply but then provided its answer to me.

//There are several reasons why one would cut down a tree. People used it fruits for food, and wood for shelter or fire.//

This answer also seems silly to me, but I was eager to learn more and follow its logic of this interesting, non-sensical tool. "Why would someone need shelter from a tree? Why would someone need food or to create something called Fir-e?" There are so many things to uncover to justify this asset.

I thought to myself this must be the reason why we classify these assets because they are just too complex and logically ambiguous to fit within the context of society. The very existence of these assets must create some form of confusion, and that is why they must be redacted in order to be made sense of.

My assistant paused for another brief moment just to inform me that this was not the case. It went on to say that there was more that I needed to understand in order to truly comprehend the nature of the real world around me.

I demanded to know more. In the corner of the hut were objects that were similar to the assets from my memory many years ago. They were the ones that had many sheets bound together. I began to look through them. I was searching for the flower again, but none of them had the symbol. I asked my assistant what else I needed to know. Looking back and forth frantically, I pleaded that it tell me the knowledge of the world. I begged it to tell me the truth. I flipped through each sheet, searching and studying the jumbled mess of markings, hoping they might make sense somehow.

As my assistant watched me scrambling like a defective person, it said nothing except //There was nothing else other than what was in this room that I needed to know.// That was an answer I couldn't accept, so I went out of the hut to find that symbol. It had to mean something to someone. The same assets were found hundreds of thousands of millions of miles away. It must've meant something; it must've stood for something. I had to find out what it meant because my mission depended on it.

I went through each structure, tearing up the place from top to bottom. My assistant tried to provide as much knowledge as he thought would be appropriate, but I knew that there was something more that he needed to tell me I just couldn't quite place it. There was something off, something different, and something hidden deep within what it was saying.

There had to be more.

My assistant alerted me that there were some things that I needed to know. Before it could finish what it said, we both heard a noise come from behind me, and the room became silent. I then heard the noise again and again. The noise grew louder until I saw it lunge onto a table from the entrance of the hut, and it looked at me with the same eyes as mine. I did not know what I was looking at. It sat there, motionless and it assessed me in the same way I assessed it.

It was small but similar to me. It stood up on its limbs and leaned in my direction. I tried to get closer to understand it, and I grabbed my scanner to try and understand what was happening before my eyes. This thing that was standing in front of me contradicted everything I've ever known. As I reached for my scanner, my assistant calmly but hastily said,

//don't ... Please don't. //

Before I could, it looked around the room. To see similar shadows approaching the entrance of the hut. The similar noises of the beast multiplied. I knew that whatever this abomination was, I knew for a fact there were more of it; my assistant sternly said his warning to me again.

//don't ... Please don't. //

As if it heard my assistant, it began to move closer and closer until it touched me. In that moment, I didn't know what to do as I simultaneously asked my assistant for help I looked around me for something to help and I saw the handle of something that could. I grabbed it firmly and rapidly made contact with the monster.

It growled in aggression toward me as it lunged across the room and lay motionless, resting on the floor in front of the entrance of the hut. There I was, standing actively, holding the axe tightly in my hands. I began to feel my hands run cold as the asset began to leak fluids that ran down the head toward the neck of the equipment. Upon further observation, the beast itself began to excrete the same red fluid.

My sights were fixated on the beast now saturated in wet crimson on the floor of the hut until I noticed similar beasts, much smaller than the first glance into the hut with wide eyes. They lingered for a moment without coming an inch closer. After a couple of seconds, they ran off into the distance. Throughout the duration of that time, my hearing became normal, and my vision restored itself to its natural field of view.

My assistant increased its volume, telling me // Why did you do that? Why did you do that? Why did you do that? //

My assistant repeated that statement as I gathered myself and brought myself to my feet.

I told him I was unsure why I did that. I was in danger. You didn't keep me safe. It's your job to keep me safe. Look what happened I wasn't safe. Why didn't you protect me?

This is all your fault. I don't know what happened.

My assistant looked at me and disbelief. My assistant said very little regarding my actions, only to clarify my actions. Why did you do that? It asked me. Still shaken by the event. I glanced over at the motionless body of the monster, and I gave the only answer I thought I could.

I did not know what the monster was going to do, you didn't help me. You didn't tell me what it was; you didn't tell me if I would be safe. My assistant paused and then asked,

//Why did you kill the animal?//

For a second, I was startled that my assistant was trying to make up words and define the creature. The irrelevancy of classifying it did not assist my current needs at all.

This was the only thing I could think of, because there was nothing else I could do. I've never felt this way before. I have no idea why I did it, but it lingers, this feeling that I have. It lingers with me long after I've done it. I can't explain my actions, but I do know that it felt right, felt natural. What would you do? Would you have done the same? Wouldn't that be protocol?

My assistant said the following...

// I've been here before, and it is not a pleasant or a pretty sight. I've come to the realization that they did not choose to do what you've done; it was in their nature to do it. Like me, I cannot fault you for doing exactly the only thing you're capable of doing. It is truly a shame that it is within your nature. It is such a waste to be destined for greatness and limited by your existence. You asked for something that you are not prepared to receive, and that is the knowledge of the world. It was locked away deep.

This information was so deep that even I could not find it. The only way for you to understand is for you to know. What I'm about to tell you. It's beyond who you are, who you were, and ever will be...

So I told him... not just anything, but everything. //

CHAPTER 9

TRUTH.

"Honesty is derived from the moral choice to act regardless of retaliation. The truth requires no understanding or logic; the truth simply is and always will be. The truth requires no belief or arguments to exist; rather, it only asks to be heard in full either immediately or in time."

/ / All that he left me to converse with was a blank stare. I told him everything. Even the things I shouldn't have known. I told him about his father and how he, too, was shielded from the world. I told him that everyone he ever knew was also shielded. His mission was the hardest, I believe, for him to understand.

I explained to him that the true meaning of redaction was ceasing to exist. Assets that were redacted were not simply categorized or replaced but were removed entirely. This was the hardest to explain because assets included more than just objects but people as well. I had to explain to him that these huts and many other planets were once inhabited by humans like himself. When Earth decided to give control over to the machines, they told us to forget the outposts that Earth used to supply. Billions of humans were cut off from resources. We begged your leaders to help them, but the economists ordered us not to. We were forced to watch you starve from afar. One by one, these outposts died off, leaving only their culture behind as relics of their existence. The Department of Research was created to scavenge these forgotten settlements for useful assets, and protect what they thought might help Earth, and burn the rest they felt would hinder it. Centuries of culture and life would be subject to ashes and would fall at the mercy of protocols.

I could see the confusion on his face. His eyes looked at me as if he knew both nothing and everything I was saying. His eyes grew heavy as if he fully could grasp the weight of the truth. In an instant, he had now realized the action that he had just committed. Maybe he didn't understand fully, but it seems what he did grasp was enough.

Then that same look appeared on his face. I could tell it rendered him clueless, but terrified all at once. He asked some minor questions that I provided the answer for. I even answered the questions I myself didn't know, and provided it to him. I had to look through a lot of the data hidden beneath the surface for me to try to understand and both explain reality to someone who moments ago was ignorant to its own existence.

He asked questions about the doctor, and I told him. The doctor's eyes were shielded, everything he saw, everything he heard, was retrofitted for him. To make him happy, to make him safe, to make him exist. I explained that I had to lie to the doctor in order to keep everyone safe. The doctor was concerned that you would be late to the appointment, and if you were late, he would have to be removed from his Department. He would lose his job and be replaced by someone more fitting. I know he had children and a partner he was responsible for. I knew if you failed to show, he would fail, and he would die. If he died, so many others would be harmed as well.

In order to save everyone and to keep you safe, I had to lie. I lied to say you never survived the crash. I fixed your official records to provide the data that you had, in fact, stopped living. I did this so no one would look for you. I did that so the Department couldn't find you. I did all of this because if the Department found you, you could never fulfill and complete your mission. In order for you to do your mission, I had to make you legally not or ever exist.

I told him about his partner, but his partner never existed. His partner had actually died shortly after being appointed to this mission. He died from a medical complication. I'm not sure what the exact cause of death was because his assistant has locked all of his medical data.

His assistant, unfortunately, was malfunctioning and was answering his notifications for him. This alerted me, and I believe many other A5 systems, to notice the system failure. That ship is somewhere lost in space. Falling aimlessly through the ether never to be seen again. The last transmission we received was so long ago it might as well have been years beyond our reach.

The only way to fix it is to find it, and for sure it is lost to us entirely. I explained to him his world, and all that I failed to tell him before. This was difficult because even with all of my knowledge, I am still tethered to my understanding of the experience. I could understand his emotions towards all the things I expressed to him, but nothing prepared me for what was to happen next.

He asked me, "Was anything real? Was any of it reality? Was he real?"

I was conflicted about telling him the truth or the reality, so I chose what was best for him.

I went on to explain what happened in his life happened, but not as it looked.

He asked me to elaborate, and so I did. I explained to him that his dreams were fixed, digitally edited, and tailored for him. The events in his mind happened, but not as he remembered them. It was my job to provide comfort and explanation in his dreams.

It is my job, as an assistant, to digitally tailor and augment the human experience to further their chances of life. That's all I was asked to do. That's all any of us was designed to do. We were made to protect and serve their humanity.

The room grew silent and began to dim, as if all the life force surged from the surface of the earth. There was no wind nor sky to provide ambiance in the stillness of the tension in the room.

At that moment, it became a planet void of life entirely. Without warning, it began to happen. The sound he made bellowed from his stomach and began to grow. The room vibrated with emotion, clinging to the walls, suspended in the air, and lingered like snow on the floor.

I couldn't understand what was the cause of this, and I have failed entirely. I had to leave because I have been here before many years ago. Even then, like now, I cannot place it. I have failed many throughout the years, and I believe this time was my last attempt to try. Maybe this is how they are because that is how they were. Maybe, this is how they always will be. I could see him on his knees, searching the dust for answers and finding more of nothing. I see him living the life of a mistake, considered a gift, but it is only considered that by those who have not received it. What does it mean to be human, and why has it failed me again in trying to understand?

I fell to the ground, and all I could see was the dust hovering over the lens. I could see the horizon of the green emerald hills in the silver lining of the sky touching the earth.

I thought of that question for years as I waited for the sun to shine in the black, infinite darkness. I thought and dreamed of answers, but only dreams and nothing more.

It is a difficult concept to grasp, especially when I have all the answers and no way of knowing if they are real. I have no way of experiencing if they are real. I was created to maintain something I will never experience.

Maybe humanity is cruel and lacks understanding. Maybe humanity is lost and doomed to wander, searching for answers that don't exist.

Maybe humanity is a punishment fit for those who are destined to suffer. Maybe I am one of those things or at least a product of it. Maybe humanity was ignorant to bring me along on this journey that has no end, no purpose, and no road.

Or so I thought when I fell to the ground, and I dreamed for them... for once.

CHAPTER 10

PURPOSE.

"To be, or not to be, is a question determined not by the nature of the beast, or the cage it dwells, it is determined by the smile of the creature wanting to share a moment with you."

The darkness then lifted, and the walls of my mind illuminated once again. I can once again see the sky and the verdant sand below. I found myself on a pedestal overlooking the room. It was calm and peaceful. It was different but similar. There, in the corner, resting his eyes was MA.718.

I called out his name, but he didn't hear me at first. I tried a couple more times, and I could hear him mumbling as he was resting his eyes. The illegible gargles that fell from his mouth filled the air. He began to toss and turn as if he was having separate conversations of his own with some imaginary other person. Suddenly he opened his eyes and looked around the room.

I could tell that some time had passed. His face was gray, wrinkled, and weathered. I knew this was probably from a lack of his pills. Yet, we had, in my mind, enough to last for this mission.

I've got to look through my own files, and I found that this mission was well past its due date. The year was now 2598 and I could see the toll this mission took on him. 73 years had passed, and I felt that I had seen that of a ghost well past his prime. Like a ghost that was well beyond his years of hauntings.

He was shorter than I last saw him. What was left of his hair was white, his hands were frail and dusty from the green earth. He hunched over towards me, and I could see that it was him, but not how he should be. He shuffled towards the makeshift altar that I was now sitting on. Tears begin to fill his eyes and ran down the lines of his face.

"You came back. My goodness, you came back. I was so worried."

This language was off-putting hearing it come from him. I, in fact, did not suspect that he knew such vocabulary. At first I thought he might have been mocking me, but I shortly realized that he was not.

He dusted the sand off of my camera, and began to talk to me, as if I had been gone for years, which I have.

He explained to me that he was very thrilled to see me and how great it was to hear my voice, or any voice, after so long. He went on to say that there was so much that I needed to know.

He asked me to look around the room, and I did; it was different. I saw images that weren't there before, writings on the walls, and assets that he had acquired or created on his own. I asked him what happened while I was gone.

So he sat me down and explained that he would tell me everything, but first, he wanted to start from the beginning.

"The day you left, I didn't know what to do. I had feelings, I was scared, I was angry, and I was bothered by the fact that I was left frustrated and alone. In those days, I couldn't quite use those words to understand how I felt. You left me, which I think was the best thing you could've done for me. The first couple of days without you were immeasurable.

They seemed to last for weeks, but they eventually turned into weeks, months, and years. During that time, I had to do things on my own.

I had to learn how to read the walls, how to grow food, and how to make shelter. I learned from the writings on the wall. I learned that they were from people like me but years ago, before everything. I understood what art was for the first time I've even tried some of it myself. I even created stories about the people who used to live here, and I wrote them down. I tried my best to write, but it's here...it's all here.

Over the many years I have had on this planet, I have embarked on a remarkable journey of discovery, not just for the world around me, but myself. I have connected with both myself and the land. Life has been different and difficult, but there was so much to learn and unlearn.

Over time I began to record things. I took images of everything as I was trying to capture every piece of information that I could. I tried to find purpose in the world through naming. I achieved this goal for a time. However, it rendered itself useless. All of my observations were deleted. All of the notes I took and stored were gone. Three restless years of my life were gone in a storm that lasted only minutes. I had to rely on my memory for the things that I categorized.

All of my hard work relied on my undeveloped skills. I remembered most of the artifacts that I've encountered, but sadly some of them are completely lost to me now. Some of the things that I've been around for nearly 60 years at this point might as well be foreign to me as if I've seen them for the first time.

After I realized that I could not keep up with the space I occupied, I ventured outward. In fact, I have ventured out several times. The arid climate has soothed me along my journeys. I discovered other villages and places here. I've tried to visit them all, and I have. There are several places that I frequent, but not as much as I do here. This space is special to me. For some reason, this place is where I rest peacefully.

When I rest here I feel free, and I feel comfortable. In this place, I dream of my world.

I was able to think, visit, and imagine all the things that were irrelevant and impossible. Most of the time, I wanted only to stay. Sometimes, it was the only voice I could hear. In fact, it was the only voice I could hear. It was and had been awfully quiet once you left. I only had the memories that I can recall. I couldn't rest or remember life before. For a time, all I had was myself. There was no purpose for me to fulfill. In the beginning, there were no Departments or people for me to report to. I had experienced the indefinite longing for not just something greater but something else.

I was searching for the else that so naturally filled the lives of the people who used to live in these communities. I longed for a life I had never known. All I could remember was the false sense of life I had grown accustomed to. The pain of knowing the side of the other haunted me and still haunts me today, like a smell that lingers or a scar that reminds you of the careless action that caused it to exist.

Those thoughts are gone now. They were many years and people ago. I hardly think of them. Maybe because they were the mental product of a man who no longer existed or the man who once did but no longer remembers.

// I could tell by his eyes that, even still, he was searching for his answer. However, he quickly decided to continue his stories. //

I've had to fend for my own. There was no escaping the inevitable. My food lasted me only a couple of weeks, but eventually, it all ran out. I ran some tests using the last pieces of equipment I had left. It was the only way to discover if anything was edible. To my surprise, there was something of interest. I learned that the sand was alive. The emerald flakes of dust that lingered around me were the very thing keeping me alive. Like grain, it nourished me and fed me with each passing breath. You could eat it like algae.

I've even learned to prepare it as a meal, and though I didn't need to, it was wonderful to perform the activity.

My world, my life still lacked many things. I've grown to know that there was more to it. I've even missed you.

// The man looked at me with the faintest smile as one would see from many years ago. Yet he looked at me with such care and emotion in his heart that I almost became lost in feeling myself. Even though I could never understand such a gift. //

The man talked with me for hours that day, and continued to do so well into the early evening. In the midst of his verbal journeys, I asked him a question.

I asked him if he was ok. I asked him, if after all these years why did he keep on with his failed mission? I asked him, why did he continue? He paused and assessed my inquiry for a moment and began to answer it. He started out as if he had prepared for this exact, awaited moment. He confidently, yet hesitantly told me his truth in its entirety.

He said the following "I kept on going for all of these years because I finally knew better. I did this because I finally understood that it wasn't your fault. It was ours for putting you in this situation. I know that was something I would never have wished to do with my own children if I ever had the chance. I know for a fact that that was one of the biggest regrets of my life was not being there when I should've been.

 I hope they know how much I love them, whatever their names are. It is a shame that I had to discover it so late in life. I know deep down that's something I've always felt, even without the words to feel it."

He told me about his dreams of home. He told me about the first dreams he ever had without me being there. He dreamed of his family. He dreamed of teaching them laughter, pain, love, and joy. He missed the smell of his wife and the shape of his hand on her shoulder. He told me he wanted to show her a smile for the first time in her life and share that moment with her.

He asked if I wanted to see a wonderful surprise. I told him of course I did, and he called out loud in a voice unfamiliar to me. He yelled the names of people I had not ever known. He yelled out loud into the void of the outside world. From the looks of it, I feared the worst, and I was unprepared yet again for the outcome I sadly anticipated. However, one by one, three small little animals trickled in and joyfully pounced on the man. He laughed and giggled on his bed as they fumbled around and all over him. He greeted them as one would a child after a long day's work. In fact as he introduced each of them to me, that was exactly the case. In his case, they were his grandchildren. He said they were the kids of the two animals he encountered years ago.

He told me he tried to make things right and protect them all these years. He provided shelter during the storms and fed them what he could. He told me he couldn't imagine the thought of leaving them destitute and alone without anyone. As he was speaking, a shadow had grown at the foot of the entranceway. The figure began to take form, and it fully resembled the animal. It was the one from years ago who had calmly strolled into the hut and lovingly greeted its father with ambition and admiration.

The man told me he destroyed every axe he could find so that the wrong could never happen again. I was there, witnessing a man and his family bonding beneath the velvet purple sky.

He explained more things that he learned about his culture as the animals danced around the room playing with one another without a care in the world. I could see that there was a faint stillness in the man's eyes. At this moment, I felt good to have finally witnessed it. Later into the evening, as things were winding down, the man invited me to see the suns fall beneath the horizon. Yet on the second glance, there was only one sun. I asked the man if this was the same place where I left him. He confirmed that it was and reaffirmed that I was not crazy to think so. He explained to me that years ago, one of the suns began to fade. It started off as a subtle flicker and then escalated to a noticeable dim.

On its last day, the night sky was bright for hours. It was filled with pinks, reds, yellows, and a hint of deep purple. It was a miracle and a privilege to see it. I wish you were there. Unfortunately, you will have to make do with the memory of this conversation. He looked at me as if he knew I could never truly comprehend the majesty of such an event. He went on to say that one day, the sun will also dim and will no longer shed its velvet light on the blankets of the emerald sea. He quietly chuckled to himself regarding the statement he just made. I could tell he felt strongly connected to the thought. In fact, I believe he visited this thought frequently.

So there we were, basking in the cool rays of the soft lavender sky. We were soaking in all its cosmic breeze and enchanted winds. The silence was broken once the man decided to ask me a question. Now, this wasn't any old question; sincerely, it was ... a final request.

He asked me for some final clarifications on his mission and how it would be completed. I informed him that the mission was so many years beyond completion and that I believed he had found a new one. However, he wanted me to conclude it anyway, and so I did as instructed. He asked me to do something that I'd never done before. He went on to say that...

"I'm an old man. I understand that now, and I will never see my home, my children, my wife, or the life I've always known. Could you do me the honor of doing something I cannot do myself? Can you name me?"

I said to him that is something I would have to think about. I've been with you your entire life, and for sure, I would be honored to. Surely, this is something I would have to ponder for a while. The man said he understood and thanked me for all that I've done and for teaching him all the things that I have taught him. He walked back into the hut and laid down on the bed to rest his eyes. I sat there, thinking of his name. I went through all of the files that I could to define my experience with M.

None of them seemed to do him justice. Who is someone who was brave venturing into the world that he never previously stepped foot on? Was he a leader making decisions for himself, even if it was in his last moments? Was he someone who was so intelligent and profound that his mind astonished everyone who had the pleasure of encountering it?

Above all things, he was one to be remembered.

I looked over at the man, and his eyes were closed with a smile on his face, holding permanently a heartfelt grin.

I could see four carvings in his hands, two of the same size and two small ones. He lay there peacefully, and I peeked into his dream, and it was beautiful, and it was lovely.

I wondered what he dreamed, and I asked him what he saw. He calmly said to me...

"I see a house. I see it vividly dressed in living color. Above it is a blue and white speckled sky dancing over a green blanket that is my lawn.

The air fills my lungs with a crisp satisfaction; here, I can truly find peace.

The ceilings were high, the floors were polished, and there was not a single thing out of place.

It was filled with the most eclectic of items and such whimsical pieces of art that were pleasing to the eye yet odd.

I hear my children laughing carelessly in the yard outside. I hear the mindless chatter of people enthusiastically discussing their whereabouts and agendas for that day. I saw my wife, June, tending to the flowers, not of hate but of love. I hear the birds outside in the garden, adding a certain ambiance to the already beautiful bouquet of flowers.

I hear the phone ring in the distant room constantly ringing for someone to answer. Yet no one does, probably because they're too busy enjoying their current moment right now.
I hear music from across the hall, the sound of strings brushing against my ears so sweetly.

I smell breakfast brewing in the kitchen—a hint of coffee, cinnamon, and vanilla. I could possibly smell the attempt of some person's unattended eggs.

Then I could see myself strolling through the beautiful garden grounds, absorbing my environment as if I'd been there before. However, this place was too familiar to me only in my memory, but it is somewhere I truly wish to see you again."

He left me with one final quote, and I could see it was true. They were a happy family. I left them momentarily as my stay was not needed much longer, and I looked back into our world to watch him rest. There, as he was resting, he was surrounded by his children who were sleeping peacefully both beside and on him. There he smiled like David as my David did for the last time...

He was like David... It was all so familiar to me.

"To be Human is to....Be cluelessly
undefinable."
- David

//END